# Barefoot

Lianne Kadakia

# Contents

# Chapter 1

"Sidney, give Penny the remote before you wake Sadie up!" I whisper-yelled to the dork I have to call my brother.

"Why should I? I had it first." He shot right back at me.

"Because I told you too and I literally just got Sadie to take her nap. You know how fussy that seven year old can get." I warned my brother for the last time.

"Fine," He mumbled and threw the remote in our sister Penny's general direction. It landed by her feet that were propped up on a pillow on the coffee table, "she always gets what she wants."

"It's because I'm older then you." Penny said with a satisfied grin as she turned on the tv.

"By ten months!" Sidney yelled.

"And sixteen days." Penny added, just like she always does.

"Both of you just shut up and stop screaming. If Sadie wakes up from one of you, you will both have to deal with me." I threatened before leaving the tiny space we call a living room. I walked into the kitchen and mentally groaned at all the dishes piled up in the sink. I got to scrubbing the glass dishes and was glad it was the last few days of summer. The younger ones would be going back to school and so will I. Senior year. I should be happy it's my senior year and I am to some extent, but I know that I have no plans for after high school except finding a full time job and staying home. It's not like I could ever afford college and I definitely wouldn't be getting any help from my pathetic excuse of a father. I'm probably not smart enough for college anyways. My grades were just slightly above average.

"I'm hungry." My second youngest sister, Polly, complained as she walked into the kitchen.

"Shit." I groaned.

"You said you'd stop swearing in front of the eleven year old." Sidney reminded me from the living room.

"Shut up." I returned. I completely forgot about dinner, I didn't realize how late it was. I turned away from Polly and opened the pantry. We only had some chips and granola bars. I yanked open the fridge next. All I saw was half a gallon of milk left, a few apples, some eggs, and what looked to be left over spaghetti. I considered the spaghetti, but then decided there wasn't enough for the five of us.

"Fuc...crap." I muttered. I walked over to the kitchen table and picked up my wallet. Opening it, I found a twenty dollar bill and some pennies.

"Pizza?" I questioned through the house. I received three replies 'yes' and knew Sadie wouldn't mind pizza when she woke up. I grabbed my crappy phone out of my pocket and dialed the local pizza place in our city, because it had the cheapest prices.

"Ya, one large half cheese, half mushroom pizza for delivery." I told the guy over the phone. After giving him the address and hanging up I decided to check on Sadie. When I walked into her room she wasn't on her bed sound asleep like I thought she would be, instead she was on the floor looking through some of Penny's teen magazines.

"Sadie, why are you looking at those?" I questioned and lightly snatched the magazine from her tiny seven year old hands. I silently prayed nothing too bad was in a teen girl magazine.

"I'm too old for naps." She said simply, only answering my question partly.

"In the mood for some pizza?" I asked, deciding to give up asking her about the magazines. I would have to tell Penny to be more careful leaving them out later. I watched as Sadie's face brightened at the mention of pizza. She nodded her head eagerly.

"It'll be here any second, go wait in the living room with everyone." I told her and watched her jump up and exit the room. I sighed and looked around the cramped room with three beds in it. One for Penny, and a bunk bed for Polly and Sadie. Our house only had three bedrooms total and with Sidney and I in one and our father in another, the three girls had to share the last one. The sharp ring of the doorbell pulled me from my thoughts.

"Pizza!" Polly and Sadie screamed together from the other room. I met my four siblings in the living room just as Penny was opening the door. I grabbed my wallet off the coffee table and met Penny at the door. I paid the boy that looked around my age as Penny eagerly grabbed the large pizza from him.

"You go to school at Frontier High right?" The boy asked me as he gave me my change for the twenty.

"Ya, I'm a senior once school starts back up." I replied.

"Me too. Maybe I'll see you around sometime." He said.

"Maybe." I answered before handing him a two dollar tip, hoping he wouldn't judge the lack of it too much. He simply smiled at me before adjusting his hat for the pizza place and stepping away from our house. I shut the door behind him and watched through the blinds as he got into the car and drove off.

"Can you stop stalking the pizza guy and come eat with us?" Penny asked me with that special sass in her voice no fifteen year old should have. I turned away from the window and joined my siblings at the table. We ate the pizza and talked about random stuff the whole time. When we finished I sent Sadie and Polly off to bed, solely for the reason that I knew the time I send them to bed and the time they actually calm down enough to sleep, are two very different times.

"Sid, help Penny with the dishes. I need to do some things." I told my only brother, "and don't complain." I warned before he had the chance to open his mouth. Instead he settled for an annoyed groan. I went back into the living room and went through all the mail piling up on the messy coffee table. I pulled out all the bills for the month and started working out the numbers.

I was halfway through figuring out where the money for the bills would come from when I saw headlights flash through the blinds.

"Dad's home." I warned Penny and Sidney, who were still in the kitchen.

"I'll be in my room." Penny announced to us and I watched as she appeared from the kitchen to the living room and disappeared up the small creaky stairs.

"Keep the two youngest in there." I told her.

"Was planning on it." She called back before I heard the door upstairs open and close. A few seconds later Sidney emerged from the kitchen and sat down next to me on the couch. He got comfortable to make it look like he's been there a while. I continued with the bills that were in my hand and didn't bother looking up as the front door swung open and slammed shut.

"I'm going to bed." My dad slurred, obviously drunk.

"Got any money left over from what you took today?" I asked, a slight edge in my voice. I knew since this afternoon that my father found the money we had saved in an old cereal box in the cabinet. Bills were due in a week and I was more mad at myself for not hiding it well enough than him finding the cash. I've learned that the most obvious places are sometimes the best and other times they are the worst.

"No." He grumbled and made his way to his room.

"Bills are due by the end of this week and unless you want to come home to a house without water or electricity after you're done getting drunk all day, you might want to reconsider your answer." I said, the edge in my voice getting stronger and more impatient. He huffed in annoyance and emptied his pockets. Throwing all the coins and cash he had before wobbling his drunk ass up the stairs. I collected the money and only counted a total of fifteen dollars and fifty cents.

"We had over sixty in that box." I complained in frustration.

"Need to find a better hiding spot." Sid said, offering no help.

"I'm running out of places to put money." I sighed.

"Well, I can have twenty by tomorrow." Sidney told me before flipping the tv on.

"How?" I asked skeptically. We lived in the worst possible side of town, I knew the types of bad things my siblings could get into.

"Some people owe some money that I have yet to get." He shrugged, looking at the tv.

"As long as you aren't selling drugs." I told him. I couldn't protect my younger siblings from everything, but I could damn well try.

"Who me? Never." He said in fake surprise. I just chuckled and calculated the rest in my head. I could probably get an advanced paycheck at work if I promise my boss to close up by myself for a few nights and I can check dad's wallet if he ever passes out drunk anywhere, which is highly probable. Penny receives her paycheck the day before bills are due, so we will just have to hope that's enough.

I'll figure something out, because my dad sure as hell won't. He hasn't helped out this family for the past seventeen years I've been alive, why would he start now?

:-:-:-:-:-:-:

"Everyone have their backpacks and lunches?" I asked my four younger siblings as they crowded around the small kitchen counter.

"Yes, we had them the first time you asked, and we have them now." Sidney said in annoyance.

"Okay, then what are you waiting for? You're gonna miss the bus." I told them as I ushered them towards the front door.

"We have ten minutes." Polly told me.

"Doesn't matter, it's the first day. The bus might come early." I knew they had ten minutes before the bus came, but I had some business to do before I left for school. I shot Penny a pleading look and she seemed to get the hint.

"Come on guys, Pax is walking to school and unless you want to be sweaty on the first day of school, we better go." She said to her three younger siblings. Sadie and Polly eagerly walked out the door. Being in second and sixth grade, the first day of school was still exciting for them. Sidney lazily followed behind them and Penny gave me a small smile before turning out the door. I stood, staring at the closed door for a minute before turning around.

I crept up the stairs as quietly as I could and stopped at the first door on the left. I strained to listen through the thin door for a minute and when I heard snoring, I turned the knob. I pushed open the door all the way with only a few squeaks along the way and stared at my fathers sleeping form. He was on his back with his one hand to his face and his other resting on his stomach. He was still in the jeans and torn t-shirt he was in yesterday when he went to bed, so I figured his wallet was on his person. I reached his bed and slowly felt his front pockets. I didn't feel anything in them so I then looked around the room. I mentally smacked myself when I saw his wallet thrown lazily on his dresser. I opened the wallet and searched its contents. He

had thirty dollars total in cash, so I decided to take ten. I closed
the wallet back up and hastily left the room.

I shoved the money in my pocket, threw my backpack over
my shoulder, and left the house. I started my walk to school
with the busy city streets surrounding me, despite it being only
8am.

# Chapter 2

I got to school with five minutes to spare. Luckily since it was my fourth year at this awful school, I knew where my first class was just by the room number on my schedule. I walked into the room right on the bell and took one of the few desks left. I sighed as I sat down and rubbed a hand down my face. School for me was just average. I had a few friends, but they were mostly just school friends. I kept quiet in class and did my work when I was given it. My sister Penny though, she could go places. She was in all honor classes and she does pretty good in them too. I was positive she could somehow figure out how to get some type of degree once she g r a d u a t - ed.

I finished my last first day like it was any other day, average. Now, I had to go back home and start living my completely not average life. All thanks to two very 'important' people in my life. The first being my mother, who came and went from our lives whenever she pleased, and the second being my dear father, who is a drunk and screwed up his life more times then me and all four of my siblings can count on our hands.

I entered my house behind my four siblings and wasn't really paying attention until I heard Penny gasp.

"Oh my god!" She screamed.

"What? What's going on?" I asked as I pushed my three other siblings to the side to be next to Penny. My eyes widened at what I saw.

Sitting on the coffee table in the living room was three huge stacks of money. They definitely weren't there when we left the house that morning.

"Where did all of this come from?" Sidney asked as he approached the money and took one of the stacks in his hands.

"These are all twenties!" He exclaimed.

"Where's dad?" Penny asked. I looked at her and realized she must have been thinking the same thing I was.

Our father did something illegal.

"Daddy!" Sadie pointed towards the man emerging from the kitchen. I felt my eyebrows shoot up when I saw him standing there. Normally at this time of day he was still out at some bar getting wasted.

"Hey, cupcake, how was school?" My dad asked Sadie with only a slight slur in his speech. He was probably only slightly buzzed.

"Good! My teacher is really nice." Sadie answered. She was still too little to fully grasp how bad our father was and I think I envied her for that. She could sense when something was off with our dad, but she was still young enough to fall for his fake sense of care and affection.

"Where did you get this money?" I asked harshly. Unlike Sadie, I lost faith in our father years ago.

"Gambling." He answered, like it was completely normal for him to come home with three large stacks of twenties.

"Gambling how?" I pushed further.

"Down at Stevie's in his back room." Stevie's was a bar down the street and I knew dad was a frequent costumer.

"Is it clean?" I asked, taking the stack Sidney was holding out of his hand.

"Of course it is! You have no faith in me, son." Dad responded, feigning being offended.

"Well, then I need this stack to pay for bills." I shook the stack I had in my hands.

"You can have half of that pile." Dad tried to grab the stack from my hand, but I pulled it out of reach.

"No way. This is probably only one-fourth of the money you've taken from us over the years, so I'm getting all of it."

"Don't you test me, boy." Dad threatened.

"Dad, I think it's time for you to go. Find some place other than here to cool off." Penny spoke up for the first time since we came home. Dad just stared at her in angry disbelief.

"Now." She pointed towards the door calmly.

Our father looked at her before glancing back at me. He huffed in annoyance before grabbing the two other stacks from the table and stumbling his way out the door.

"Why did you make daddy leave?" Sadie questioned after the door shut.

"Because he was being a meany to Pax and Penny." Polly explained to our youngest sibling, "let's go play in our room."

I watched Polly lead Sadie up the stairs and let out a breath when I heard their door click shut.

"How much do you think is in that?" Penny gestured towards the money in my hand.

"I don't know, maybe four hundred." I guessed.

"That'll definitely help us with bills this month and next months groceries." Penny said gratefully.

"Do you really think he got it gambling though?" Sidney asked while plopping down on the couch.

"I don't know that either, but I have to hope he did." I sighed.

"Well, just make sure you find a better hiding spot this time than a cereal box." Sidney joked.

"Very funny." I muttered, "I have to be at work in twenty minutes, so you have dinner tonight, Penny."

"Okay. When will you be home?" She asked.

"I have to close tonight, so most likely at midnight." I answered.

Penny just nodded in response and I quickly shoved the stack of money in my book bag before slinging it over my shoulder and leaving the house. I figured until I found a good hiding place later, the safest place for the money would be with me at work.

I walked all the way to the bowling alley where I work. I got the job when I was fourteen, because my manager knew the tough situation I was in for my family. Not a lot of employers hire people under sixteen, so I am lucky my boss was so kind and willing to make an exception.

"Hi, Linda." I greeted my boss when I walked in.

"Hello, Paxton. How are you doing, honey?" Linda greeted me.

"I'm getting through the day." I answered truthfully. Like I said, Linda knew my situation, so there was no use lying to her. Plus, it was nice to have someone outside of my family to express my concerns to and get stuff of my chest. At home, I had to be the strong older brother, but at work I could pretend to just be a teenager with an after school job.

Linda just hummed in response to my answer.

I put my book bag in my staff locker and made sure it was sealed shut before grabbing my uniform. I slipped on the polo shirt all employees are required to wear over the plan white tee I already had on and signed in at the register.

"Where do you want me today?" I asked Linda. The two of us were the only ones working, because weeknights weren't usually too busy. Just the occasional league or people who come in to practice.

"Register, shoes, and lane duty." Linda gave me my responsibilities for the night.

I nodded my head to show I understood and watched as Linda made her way to her office. After she was in her office with the door shut, I observed the bowling alley. Only two of the eighteen lanes were in use. An old couple occupied one of them and a middle age man who was definitely really good at bowling was at the other. The bowling alley is the only one in the area, so we get people from all the different parts of town.

I sat behind the counter for about an hour before the chimes on the door rang. I glanced up and noticed a group of five teenagers walking in. I didn't immediately recognize any of them, but I was sure they went to my school since Frontier High was the only high school in our city. As they walked up to me at the counter, I noticed there was two girls and three boys making up the party.

"Welcome to Linda's Lanes, will you be buying games or time today?" I asked in my costumer service voice.

"We want two games for the five of us." One of the boys spoke for everyone.

I clicked two games for a group of five into the register and checked the total. "That'll be eighty dollars in total or sixteen per person."

I collected sixteen dollars from each of the teenagers and placed the money in the register.

"You will be at lane eleven. What shoe sizes can I get all of you?" I slide down to the shoe area behind the counter.

"I'll have a size twelve."

"Nine."

"Ten."

"I'll have a size six."

"Size seven for me, please."

I grabbed all the shoes and placed them on the counter for each of them to grab. "Will you be wanting bumpers?"

"Oh, yes please." One of the girls spoke up.

"Come on, Kathrine. You always want bumpers." One of the guys complained.

"Because I need them!" Kathrine argued back.

"Well not today. I'm gonna help teach you to not rely on the bumpers." The boy promised Kathrine.

"So, thanks, but we're good." One of the other boys said to me before they all walked off towards their lane.

I occasionally watched the group of teenagers with little interest as my shift went on. Watching them laugh and smile as Kathrine pouted every time her ball went into the gutter and cheer every time one of the boys got a strike made me wonder what it was like to have friends you could hang out with outside of school on a random school night. Hanging out together looked so normal to them and I felt slightly jealous for not getting to have a normal childhood like they do. I then cursed myself mentally for even thinking like that, because my siblings needed me to be a parental figure to them. I'm giving up my childhood in hopes that they might be able to have a good future.

After the group finished their two games they brought their shoes back to me at the counter and left. No new people came in to bowl, so I didn't have anything to really do. I decided with only a half an hour left of my shift that I would get a head start on cleaning up. I started with all of the tables surrounding the lanes and then moved onto the floors. I was about halfway done when Linda came out of her office to start counting the register. Once she was satisfied that the amount the register said should be there was in fact all accounted for, she grabbed her bag and bid me a goodbye.

I watched as she locked the door behind her, so that I could get out later, but no one could get in from the outside. I finished cleaning the floors, counters, and shoes in about half an hour. I then changed out of my uniform, took my book bag from my locker, and after checking that the money was still safely zipped up, headed out myself.

The night air was a comfortable temperature and I tried to enjoy the nice weather, because I knew it would start to get colder soon as fall came around.

I made it home in fifteen minutes and noticed almost all of the downstairs lights in the house were on. I grew worried as

I approached the house, because it was almost midnight and everyone should be in bed. I pushed open the screen door and let it shut behind me. I didn't see anyone in the living room or the kitchen despite both the lights being on. I groaned in annoyance before shutting them both off and heading up the stairs. All my siblings know the importance of turning the lights off in unoccupied rooms, so our electric bill doesn't increase. I guess they don't always remember.

I made my way towards my room in the dark, because I didn't want to wake up Sidney. As my eyes adjusted to the darkness of the room I glanced at Sidney's bed and noticed he wasn't in it. I crossed the hall to the girls room and peaked inside. Sure enough, Sidney was sprawled out on Penny's bed and Penny was sharing Sadie's bed.

I smiled sadly at my sleeping siblings before going back across the hall into my room and settling into bed. I would have to ask Penny what happened tomorrow morning, because Sidney only slept in the girls' room when I'm not home and dad came home angry drunk.

I just prayed he didn't do anything too rash in front of the little ones.

# Chapter 3

"Sadie, you have to finish all of your food. We can't afford to let it go to waste." I gently scolded the tiny seven year old. We were all at the table eating breakfast and I noticed Sadie hadn't touched her plate in a while.

"I'm full." She said as she pushed the plate away from her.

"How about two more big bites and then next time I won't make you as many?" I urged her to eat just a little bit more.

She looked at me and then down at her discarded plate before making up her mind to listen to me. She scooped up a spoonful of her scrambled eggs and shoved them in her mouth. She chewed it slowly, like the taste was unbearable, but managed to swallow it all down.

"All done." She tried.

I shook my head at her, "Our deal included two bites."

She let out a sigh before scooping up another spoonful and forcing it down.

"Good job, now go get dressed for school." I instructed. Sadie followed my instructions and bounced up the stairs to her room. Polly and Sidney finished shoveling down their eggs before going to get dressed too. That left me at the kitchen table with Penny.

"What happened last night?" I asked. Penny didn't need to ask me to clarify. She knew I was talking about our father and Sidney sleeping in the girls' room the previous night.

"Dad came home drunk of course, but he kept insisting Sid knew where the money you took was. We kept telling him that you had it with you at work, but he didn't believe us. Sidney was afraid he would barge into his room in the middle of the night, so I told him he could have my bed." Penny explained.

I sighed and looked at Sadie's abandoned plate of eggs on the table, "He didn't harm anyone right?"

"No," Penny quickly said, "of course not."

Our dad was an angry drunk, but he was verbal in his abuse not physical. He's never laid a hand on any of us, but I was always afraid that the day would eventually come when he did. I just hoped it was me and not one of my siblings.

"Do you want the rest of her eggs?" I asked Penny, motioning towards Sadie's plate. Penny shook her head at me and got up from the table. I watched as she cleaned her dishes and then went up the stairs to get changed for school.

I took the remaining three bites of Sadie's eggs and washed all of our plates off in the sink before heading upstairs myself.

I pulled on some black jeans, a simple gray tee, and picked my book bag up off the floor. I decided I would keep the money with me again today until I had time to sit and think of putting it somewhere dad wouldn't be able to find. By the time I made my way back downstairs, my four siblings were all packed up and ready to go.

"Okay, I have to work right after school today, but I'll be home by eight. Penny works from three to nine, so dinner is on you tonight Sid. I think there is some macaroni and cheese boxes in the pantry you could make for the girls." I gave everyone the day plan.

"Boxed macaroni it is." Sidney faked his enthusiasm.

"Sadie, I better hear from Sid that you ate all of your mac and cheese, deal?" I crouched down to her height so she could see my face clearly.

"Deal." She muttered half-heartedly. I ruffled her hair lightly before standing back up to my full height.

"Okay, let's go everyone." I ushered everyone out the door as the big yellow school bus rounded the corner onto our street.

-:-:-:-:-:-:-:-:-:-:-:-:-

It was finally the last period of the day and I was so over it. It was the second day of school, so teachers were starting to actually give out assignments. My last class of the day was English and when I walked in the room the teacher had a seating chart posted on the board. I found my name and took my new assigned seat. My desk was near the window which

I was grateful for. I could see the board easily and also had a view of the track and baseball fields in the school yard.

I paid no attention to the person who sat down in the desk next to me until they tapped my shoulder. I glanced over at the person and could vaguely recognize him, but wasn't sure from where.

"You're the guy I delivered pizza to the other night." He said and I instantly remembered him. He looked different in regular clothes, more casual. I noticed his hair was a floppy brown mess on the top of his head that his pizza cap covered the first time I saw him. I don't remember seeing him in this class yesterday, but we didn't have our seats yet and to be honest I didn't really pay much attention.

"Half cheese and half mushroom, right?" He asked. I was slightly shocked he would remember our pizza order when he probably makes dozens of deliveries each night.

"Yeah, my two youngest sisters hate mushrooms, so we only get half." I told him.

"I'm going to have to side with your sisters on this one. Mushrooms are gross." He responded. I just answered by giving him an appalled look to which he just chuckled quietly at.

"I'm Daniel, but everyone calls me Danny."

"Paxton." I replied. Danny opened his mouth to say something, but the sharp ring of the bell shut him up. As our teacher started talking at the front of the classroom, Danny pulled out a piece of paper and scribbled something down. He then slide the paper on my desk and turned his attention back to our teacher.

"Nice to 'officially' meet you, Paxton." The note read. I looked back over at Danny, but all of his attention was focused on our teacher.

I shoved the paper in my bag and stared out the window for the rest of class.

-:-:-:-:-:-:-:-:-:-:-

"Hi, Linda." I greeted as I walked into the bowling alley. The smell of shoe cleaner and lane oil instantly bombarded my nose.

"Hello, Paxton. How are you t—," Linda's greeting was cut short by a high pitched voice.

"Paxton!" Linda's five-year-old daughter, Gracie, screamed as she ran towards me. I swooped her up in my arms and twirled us around once.

"How's little Gracie doing today?" I asked with her still in my arms.

"Good." She giggled.

"Did you start kindergarten yet?"

"No, but mommy said soon." Gracie answered. I looked over at Linda behind the counter.

"The school decided to start the kindergarteners two weeks after all the other kids this year, so everything is calm when they first go." Linda explained. I nodded in understanding.

I set Gracie down and watched as she ran off into Linda's office. I made my way to my locker, locked my book bag in, and slipped on my uniform.

"Ryan is working late tonight, so I had to bring Gracie." Linda told me after I signed into the register. Ryan is Linda's husband and it wasn't unusual that Gracie would hang out at the bowling alley when he worked late.

I nodded at her and scanned the bowling alley. Today, only one lane was in use by a lady who seemed to be practicing for a league or something.

"Slow day?" I asked Linda.

"Very," she sighed, "It is Wednesday though, so Robert's little league should be here at six."

"Okay, anything in particular you want me to do?"

"I have to crunch some numbers in my office, so can you just keep an eye on Gracie?" She requested.

"Of course."

"You're an angel, Paxton." Linda praised. I just gave her a tiny smile and watched as she turned towards the direction of her office.

A few seconds later Gracie came running out, her little ponytail swaying back and forth.

"Mommy says you have to play with me." She said.

I laughed, "Oh, did she?"

Gracie nodded her head enthusiastically.

"Okay, how about we go see how many different color bowling balls there are?" I suggested.

"The blue ones first?" She asked.

"Sure." Gracie grabbed my hand and I chuckled at her excitement as we made our way over to the bowling ball racks.

My shift went by pretty fast since I had Gracie there to keep me entertained. The little league showed up at six and Ryan arrived by seven to take Gracie home. At eight I changed out of my uniform and grabbed my book bag from my locker. Then, bidding Linda goodbye, I left the bowling alley.

I noticed the car wasn't in the driveway when I got home which meant dad wasn't home yet. Sidney and the two youngest were in the living room when I walked in.

"Simon says...jump up and down." Sidney commanded from his seat on the couch. I watched in amusement as Polly and Sadie jumped up and down like little bunnies.

"Go give Paxton a hug." Sidney commanded next. Sadie quickly ran over to me at the door and gave me a big embrace.

"Sadie, he didn't say 'Simon Says'!" Polly pointed out.

"Oh no, that means I lose!" Sadie complained.

I laughed as realization of what just happened to her set in, "Hey, you win in my book for giving me a hug."

"It doesn't matter," She sulked, "I always lose 'Simon Says'."

I ruffled her hair before looking at Sidney, "Is there any leftover macaroni?"

"In the refrigerator." Sidney replied, flipping on the tv.

I pulled the foil covered macaroni out of the fridge once I was in the kitchen and dished some out onto a plate. After making sure there was still enough left for Penny when she got home, I put my plate in the microwave. When it was finished, I took a seat at the table and started to eat. As I was eating, I tried to think of good places I could stash the money I still had hidden in my book bag.

The empty cereal box wouldn't work anymore and I concluded that would also then go for everything else in the kitchen. My room was off limits too and so was the girls'. We've all come home before to our rooms completely torn up from dad searching for anything valuable.

Once I finished my macaroni and cheese, I started walking around the house seeing if any good spots stuck out to me. Under the couch cushions was too risky. Laundry hamper had a chance of accidentally going through the wash. I even considered hiding the cash in dad's room for a split second before realizing just how stupid that idea was.

I ended up not finding a spot and gave up on my search after twenty minutes. The safest place I could think of to keep the money out of my dads greedy hands was my book bag. That way I could always have it and not have to worry about where it might be.

My only job now was to keep tabs on that book bag.

# Chapter 4

"This year we are going to focus a lot on Shakespeare's works and essay writing to prepare you for college." Mrs. Anderson explained to the class.

It was eighth period on a Friday, so everyone in the class was already mentally checked out for the weekend, myself included.

"I always start the year off by reading Macbeth, but this year I want to try something new." She continued. I was only half listening to the words she was saying. My attention was focused on the bright green grass on the baseball fields outside the window.

A tap on my shoulder pulled me from my gazing. I turned towards Danny and saw him looking at me expectedly. He must've asked me something, but I didn't hear him, so I just gave him a confused look.

"Do you want to be partners?" He repeated.

"Partners for what?" I asked, completely lost.

"While you were daydreaming over there, Mrs. Anderson said our assignment is to read Macbeth with a partner and collaborate on review questions." Danny explained.

"For how long?" I questioned. I knew Macbeth was a play, so that meant it had to be pretty lengthy.

"We have three weeks to read, answer questions, review for the test, and write an essay about the main characters tragic flaw." Danny gave me the rundown of the assignment.

"That's a lot of work." I muttered.

"That's why she is letting us work in partners. So, want to be partners?" Danny circled back to his original question.

I glanced around the room and noticed everyone else was already sitting with desks pushed together in groups of two. Danny was the only person I knew in the class and at this point was really the only option left.

I looked back at Danny, "Sure."

"Great, but can we start on Monday? My brain can't take anymore thinking today."

"Yeah, I'm over today too." I agreed. Danny smiled at me and sat back in his chair. We then spent the rest of the class making small talk and pretending to work whenever Mrs. Anderson walked by our desks.

-:-:-:-:-:-:-:-:-:-:-:-:-:-

"Can we please get bumpers on lane six?" A lady asked me from the other side of the counter.

"Of course, I'll be right over." I answered. She gave me a toothy smile before turning on her heel and walking back to her kids.

I grabbed the pole we used to push up the lane bumpers from behind the counter and made my way over to lane six.

"Mom, I don't want the bumpers. Grandpa told me that was cheating." The young boy at the lane complained.

"I'm sorry Jake, but your sister needs them, so we are putting them up." The mother replied.

I hooked the bottom of the pole into the side of the bumper and pulled up. Both bumpers shot up with a loud clunk and clicked into place.

"Thank you." The mom said to me as I was leaving.

"You're welcome, ma'am."

I claimed my spot behind the counter and looked at all the people in the bowling alley. Saturday's are the busiest day of the week and almost all of the lanes were occupied.

"Why am I always the one stuck hosting the birthday parties?" Hannah, my coworker, questioned as she joined me behind the counter.

"Because you work best with kids." I replied.

"I told Linda I liked working the parties once and now that's all she has me do." Hannah put her head in her hands dramatically.

"How many do we have today?" I asked, rubbing her shoulder comfortingly.

"Two right now, but both maxed out their capacity of twelve kids. That's twenty-four children running around with sugar highs from cake." Hannah said.

"Just be happy you aren't the one who will have to clean all their stinky shoes later." I countered.

Hannah lifted her head up to look at me with squinted eyes, "One of them growled at me, Paxton. A kid growled at me."

I chuckled, but it was quickly cut off when Hannah smacked my arm.

"I need to get back." She shuddered.

She tightened her ponytail and pushed up her glasses before heading back off in the direction of the parties.

"Good luck!" I called after her.

"Excuse me, sir?" An older lady hobbled up to the counter.

"How may I help you, ma'am?" I asked, kindly.

"My granddaughter accidentally got a ball stuck halfway down the lane." She explained.

"I'll be right there to get that for you." I told her with a smile. She smiled back before hobbling back towards her lane.

After I retrieved the ball from the lane, my shift got quiet. People came in to bowl fairly often, but we never ran out of lanes. It was currently eleven and I was behind the counter cleaning shoes. I glanced up as the door chime rung and recognized the group that walked in. The same five teenagers from earlier this week made their way over to the register. I was slightly surprised to see them here twice in the same week, but there also wasn't many other places in our city for teens to hang out.

"Are we paying for time or games, tonight?" I asked the group.

"One hour, but there will be six of us." The same boy who spoke for the group last time informed me.

"Okay, do you want to wait for them to show up or will one of you be paying for them?"

"Oh, there he is." The girl I remember being named Kathrine pointed towards the door.

My eyes widened slightly as Danny walked through the door and made his way over to his friends.

He gave them each a quick greeting and turned towards me, "Oh, hey Paxton. I didn't know you worked here."

"Uh, yeah, I do." I responded.

"Cool." Danny said and then turned his attention back to his friends, "So, how many games we playing?"

"They close at midnight, so we thought we could buy an hour." Kathrine said.

"Sounds good."

"That'll be sixty all together or ten per person." I told the group after I finished punching it into the register.

All six of them paid separately and I shut the register before asking for shoe sizes.

"I'm going to be putting you on lane two. Would you like bumpers?" I asked as I handed them each their shoes.

"No, thanks." One of the boys said before they all headed in the direction of their lane.

I silently glanced at Danny with his friends every so often. His relaxed behavior told me he was really good friends with all of them. He wore a smile basically the entire time they bowled.

At eleven-thirty Linda emerged from her office with a coat on and an umbrella in her hand.

"It's really coming down out there." She observed. I nodded and looked at the front door. The glass had been covered in water droplets ever since it started raining fifteen minutes ago. I hoped it stopped by midnight, so I wouldn't have to walk home in the pouring rain.

"Have a goodnight, Paxton. Don't forget to shut the lights off and lock the door." Linda reminded me.

"I will, goodnight." I waved at her as she left the bowling alley. I stared at the door after it shut behind her, just watching the water droplets slowly slide down the glass.

The crashing of pins brought my attention back to the lanes. The only two groups of people left were three middle-aged men that were packing up their gear and Danny's friend group.

"That's my fourth strike this game, suck it." One of the boys taunted.

"Oh shut up, Brian. Just because you took lessons when you were nine does not mean you are better than us." Kathrine said, crossing her arms.

My view of the group was cut off when the three men brought their shoes up to me at the counter. I collected the shoes and started spraying them with cleaner. At about ten minutes till closing, Danny and his friends left. I started cleaning their six pairs of shoes too when the door swung back open.

"I'm sorry, we're clos—." I stopped mid-sentence when I saw the person who just walked in was Danny.

"Oh, did you forget something?" I asked him.

He shook his head at me as he walked over to the counter, "I noticed there aren't any more cars left in the parking lot except mine. Do you have a ride home?"

I was taken aback by his question and took a few seconds to form a response, "Oh, um, I usually just walk home after my shift. I only live like fifteen minutes away walking distance."

"At midnight? That can't be safe, plus it's pouring outside." Danny's face expressed a look of concern. My eyes darted back over to the entrance and sure enough the rain was still falling hard on the glass door.

"Yeah, well I don't have a car, so walking is my only option." I shared my limited options with him.

"Well tonight you have more than one option. Let me drive you." Danny offered.

I instantly shook my head, "No, I can't ask you to do that."

"I offered, so technically you didn't ask." He corrected me.

"I won't be ready for another forty-five minutes. I have to cleanup." I tried to explain.

"I don't have anywhere to be."

I looked at Danny with disbelief. What teenager would want to wait around this late on a Saturday night in an empty bowling alley?

"You don't hav—." I tried to reason with him again.

"I want to." He assured me, "Besides I can't have you getting sick from walking out in the rain and missing school. I'm not reading Macbeth all alone."

"Oh, so this is just insurance that I'll do half of our English assignment?" I chuckled.

"Maybe." Danny joked back as he took a seat to wait.

I finished cleaning all the shoes, mopped the floor, and shut down all the lanes in record speed, because I felt bad for holding up Danny.

"I just have to change out of my uniform then I'll be ready." I told Danny. He nodded briefly at me before looking back down at his phone. I went into the back to take off my polo shirt. I then opened my locker and shoved the shirt in. Finally, I grabbed my book bag, checked quickly to see the money was still there, and met Danny. I paid the bills yesterday and ended up having some money left over that I was saving until I went grocery shopping tomorrow.

"Ready?" Danny asked, standing up. I nodded and followed him out the door. Once we were both through, I turned around and rotated the lock until I heard the click. I tried to pull it open and was satisfied when it didn't budge. We lightly jogged to the car to try and stay as dry as possible. I slid into the passenger seat as Danny got in the drivers side.

The drive was pretty quiet. We only really spoke when I told Danny which way to turn. As we pulled into the driveway, I was surprised to see it was empty. Normally, dad would be home by now as it was nearly one in the morning.

I clicked my seatbelt off and swung my book bag over my shoulder before opening the door.

"Thanks for the ride." I crouched down to look in the door as I talked to Danny.

"No problem. See you at school on Monday." He responded.

"See you." I said as I shut the car door and made my way up to the front door. Once I was inside I went to shut the door and noticed Danny was still in the driveway. I closed the door all the way and only then he put his car in reverse and left.

I smiled to myself.

He waited to make sure I was safe inside before leaving.

# Chapter 5

"Can I get your number, so we can text any questions we have about the assignment?" Danny asked me about five minutes before the end of class on Monday.

"Uh, sure." I responded and handed my phone to Danny to add a new contact.

"Woah, you only have like three contacts in here." Danny commented. I felt my face heat up at his words and instantly felt embarrassed. It was true, I only had a phone number for my dad, my mom, and Penny. Dad's phone was a cheap, flip phone that he never used and I can't even remember the last time I called him. I'm not even sure if my mom's phone number is still a valid number to reach her on. And Penny is the only other person in my family to have a smart phone like me, because we both pay for them out of our job paychecks.

When I didn't say anything to Danny's comment, he quickly typed in his contact information and handed me my phone back.

"Text me something real quick, so I can add your number in my phone." He instructed. I selected his contact name and sent him a simple 'Hey'. His phone quickly buzzed with my message and he replaced the number with my name.

"Great," Danny clicked his phone off at the same time the bell rang, "See you later."

"Bye." I replied and watched him leave the classroom. I collected my papers, shoved them in my book bag, and left the room also.

-:-:-:-:-:-:-:-:-:-:-:-:-:-

"You have to solve for x by subtracting six from both sides and then dividing both sides by five." I explained to Polly. She came to me about five minutes ago confused on her math homework.

"I just don't get why they have to put letters in math when numbers are hard enough." She complained. I chuckled slightly at her agitation and didn't have the heart to tell her that it gets so much worse.

"Do you at least understand how to solve the problems now?" I asked. She nodded before writing down the answer to the problem and showing me the paper.

"Yes, that's right. Now, try the other ones." I told her and got up from the couch to go start on dinner. I only had to make enough for three tonight, because Penny was working and got a free meal every shift and Sidney was spending the evening at a friends house.

I was busy boiling the water to make pasta when my phone dinged. I picked it up expecting a text from Penny, but Danny was the one who sent a message.

Can you translate Shakespeare's text?

I almost laughed out loud at his question, because we both spent the whole time in class earlier today just trying to understand what we were reading.

I typed back and sent him a message, I speak English, not Shakespeare.

As I waited for him to text back, I poured the pasta noodles into the boiling water.

How are we supposed to answer questions when we don't even know what we are reading? Danny texted.

We guess. I replied.

Do you think I could come over, so we can work on it? Maybe if we are reading it together some of it will make sense.

I instantly started panicking. I couldn't have Danny come over. No one ever comes over to our house. I was also making dinner and had to watch Polly and Sadie. Plus, I didn't even want to think of what would happen if Danny was over and dad came home. I finally had someone at school who seemed to enjoy talking to me and didn't judge me, because he didn't really know my situation. If Danny came to the house he could figure out how screwed up my life was and might not want to talk to me again. I refused to ruin the one potential real friend I could have in the near future.

I hastily typed, I have to watch my little sisters tonight and they might be distracting.

Oh, I won't get distracted. My house is always loud. I stared anxiously at my phone. This was not the direction this conversation was supposed to be heading.

Well, we still have to eat dinner. I made another excuse.

I can come later. Does seven sound good? Danny asked. I groaned at my phone before sighing in defeat. He wasn't going to give up no matter how many excuses I made.

Seven works. I texted back after hovering my finger over the send button for a minute.

See you then.

I set my phone down and took the pot of pasta off the stove. After draining the hot water into the sink, mixing in the sauce, and dishing out three platefuls of pasta, I sat down at the table.

"Girls! Dinner!"

-:-:-:-:-:-:-:-:-:-:-:-:-

I was anxiously scrubbing dishes when I heard a knock on the front door. After we ate dinner, I suggested Polly and Sadie go to their room. I told them I was having a friend over for a school project and that I would appreciate it if they weren't too loud.

I dried my hands off with a towel before answering the door.

"Hey." Danny greeted from the front stoop. He had his book bag slung over his shoulder and a small smile on his face.

"Hey, come in." I stepped aside, so he could enter the house. Danny's eyes immediately started scanning the interior of the house probably just to get a feel of the space, but I couldn't help but feel self-conscious. Danny was the first person other than family over our house in a long time, so the whole situation felt strange.

"We can work in here on the couch or in the kitchen at the table." I gave Danny our two options.

Danny glanced over at the couch, "In here works."

"Okay, you can get set up. I just have to go up to my room and grab my book bag." I said. He nodded and went over to the couch as I made my way up the stairs to my room. I grabbed my book bag from off my bed and joined Danny downstairs.

"We just had dinner, but I can get you a snack or a drink if you want?" I offered. Danny was already sitting on the couch with his papers all over the coffee table and his copy of Macbeth open in his hands.

"No, I'm good. Thanks though." He replied. I sat down beside him on the couch and pulled out all of my papers along with my book too.

"So, I tried to read act one, scene two on my own, but I just couldn't understand the language." Danny said.

"Okay, then let's try reading it together."

Danny nodded in agreement and started reading the scene out loud. We worked for about an hour just trying to translate the writing style and got about half the questions for the scene done.

"Three weeks is not long enough for this much work." Danny complained after shutting his book and calling it quits for the night.

"I agree." I sighed and slumped down on the couch.

"Hey, could I have some water?" Danny asked while collecting his papers.

"Sure." I pushed myself up from the couch and stepped into the kitchen. I got a glass down from the cabinet and filled it with water from the tap. I heard the door slam open and checked the clock on the oven. It was too early for Penny to be home and Sidney was going to call me from his friends phone before he left. I was about to call out to ask who it was when a voice cut me off.

"Who are you?" Dad demanded. I felt my stomach drop as I rushed back into the living room.

"Dad, this is Danny. He's a friend from school. We were working on our assignment." I explained before Danny had a chance to speak.

"You didn't ask me if you could have a friend over." Dad said and I winced at the evident slur in his voice.

"You weren't home." I stated, timidly. I didn't want to get dad mad, but it was true that he wasn't home and plus he didn't really care that Danny was over. He just needed something to get angry at.

"This is my house which means I get to decide who comes and goes." Dad said very loudly. I wanted to laugh in his face at his comment. He might've bought the house years ago, but Penny and I were the ones paying the bills every month. Without us, my dad would be homeless.

"Please keep it down. The girls are upstairs." I settled on saying instead. The last thing anyone needed was the girls hearing us and coming out of their room. I was trying to stay calm, but knowing that Danny was watching the whole interaction with my dad right beside us on the couch was nerve-wracking.

"Polly! Sadie!" Dad's scream seemed to shake the whole house. I heard the girls bedroom door open quickly and soon they were at the bottom of the stairs taking in the scene in front of them.

"Yeah, dad?" Polly asked, but she was looking at me for an explanation. I just shrugged sympathetically and turned to our dad.

"Did you know Paxton was having someone over?" Dad questioned the girls.

"Yeah, he's Pax's friend." Sadie chirped.

"Okay, cupcake. Do you think Pax should've invited his friend over without telling me?" Dad mimicked the way Sadie said my name.

"Dad, where are you going with this?" I intervened. There was no reason to bring the girls down here to ask ridiculous questions.

"First, you bring a stranger into my house without my permission and now you are going to question me!" Dad screamed.

I flinched at his harsh voice and watched as Sadie hid herself behind Polly.

"I'm sorry, Mr. Meyers. It was my idea to come over. I think it's best if I head out now." Danny spoke for the first time since dad entered.

"Yeah, you think?" Dad huffed sarcastically.

"I'll walk you out." I hastily told Danny. I just needed an excuse to get out of the same room as my dad right now.

Danny just nodded at me and collected all of the items he brought. As I followed him out the front door, I motioned to Polly to take Sadie back upstairs.

"Our conservation isn't over, boy." Dad said right before I let the door shut behind me.

Danny stopped on the stoop and turned around to face me, "Paxton, I'm—,"

"I'm so sorry you had to witness that." I cut him off. Danny's eyes just widened at my apology and I looked at the ground in embarrassment.

"You're sorry?" He questioned, "I'm the one who should be sorry."

My head whipped back up to look at him, "What are you sorry for? My dad was the one that caused a scene."

"Yeah, because of me. You tried to stop me from coming over, but I didn't listen." Danny said.

"Well, you couldn't have known." I muttered.

"Known what?" His face changed from guilt to confusion.

"That my life was s-so...so screwed up." My voice failed me during my confession, but I maintained eye contact with Danny.

"Hey," Danny took a step towards me, "Your dads actions have nothing to do with you as a person."

I couldn't respond to that, so I just gave him a smile of gratitude. Danny just showed me that he wasn't going to judge me based on my home life. I was always so afraid of having any friends, because of the way they would react when they found out about my dad and how I was practically raising my siblings. And although tonight wasn't the ideal first impression of my house I wanted Danny to have, I knew he wouldn't stop talking to me over my alcoholic father.

"Your little sisters seem sweet." Danny changed the subject.

I smiled, "Yeah, Polly is very logical and down to earth while Sadie is very bubbly and energetic, but they are both amazing kids."

"Well, I should get going." He stepped away from me, "See you at school tomorrow."

"See you at school." I repeated and watched Danny get into his car. I watched his car back out of the driveway and ride down the street until it disappeared from my vision. I then turned around and stared at the front door.

It was time to face dad's drunken wrath.

# Chapter 6

"Then Dad finished yelling at Pax and wobbled upstairs before passing out." Polly said. She was at the kitchen table with Penny and Sidney and was explaining what happened yesterday night with Dad.

"All because your friend came over?" Penny turned to ask me.

"Yes, so learn from my mistake and don't bring any friends over." I said.

"Who was it anyway? You never hang out with people." Sidney remarked.

"His name is Danny and we were just working on a school assignment. Now can we stop talking about it?" I shoved my soggy cereal into my mouth.

"Okay, fine." He replied.

"Sadie, come eat breakfast before school!" I yelled throughout the house.

"Is she even up?" I asked my three siblings when I didn't get a reply.

"I woke her up before I came down. Maybe she fell back asleep." Polly said.

We didn't have to wonder any longer, because Sadie walked into the kitchen still in her pajamas.

"Why aren't you dressed for school?" I asked.

"I feel funny." She replied. I instantly got up and crouched down beside her. Upon closer look, I realized she was visibly shaking.

"Are you hot?" I asked. She nodded, so I placed the back of my hand on her head. Her forehead was really warm.

"She's got a fever." I announced.

"I'll call her school." Penny offered, before grabbing her phone and leaving the kitchen.

"Guess you're staying home today." I told Sadie.

"No, I like school!" She complained.

"Give it a few years, then you'll hate it." Sidney piped up from the table.

I chuckled slightly and turned back to Sadie, "You can go back to school as soon as you feel better."

"Okay." She sighed.

"How about you go watch some tv in the living room?" I suggested. Sadie listened to me and made her way into the living room.

"You gonna leave her here by herself?" Sidney asked once the tv clicked on.

"No, I'll stay with her. I need to keep an eye on that fever in case it gets worse." I said.

"I would gladly stay home and watch her instead." He offered.

"Yeah right. You're going to school." I shut down his idea of skipping real quick.

"Speaking of school, bus will be here in five." Penny said as she came back into the kitchen.

Sidney and Polly got up from their seats with their dishes. I watched as they cleaned their bowls in the sink and left to grab their book bags. I bid the three of them goodbye and listened for the front door to slam shut. The only sound left in the house was the voices coming from Sadie's cartoon. I decided to clean off my bowl too, before heading upstairs to change into a white tee and some gray sweatpants. If I was going to be home all day, I was going to dress comfortably.

I made my way back downstairs and joined Sadie in the living room, "Are you hungry?"

Sadie shook her head, "I'm super hot."

"Okay, let me check that temperature." I said and turned on my heel to go into the bathroom. I found the old thermometer we've had forever and clicked it on. I then sat down beside Sadie and instructed her to open her mouth. I waited for the beep and pulled it out before looking at the tiny screen.

"One hundred and one point four." I read.

"Is that bad?" Sadie asked.

"No, we will only worry if it gets higher." I said. Satisfied with my answer, Sadie turned her attention back to her cartoon. I sat back on the couch and started watching the program too.

About thirty minutes later, I heard footsteps descending the stairs. The footsteps halted at the bottom as Dad noticed Sadie and I on the couch.

"What are you two doing here?" He asked. I instantly noticed the lack of a slur in his voice. Normally I'm either at school or working when he wakes up, so I only ever hear his after drinking voice.

"Sadie has a fever, so we both stayed home." I explained.

"She couldn't stay by herself?" He questioned.

I looked at him incredulously, "She's seven."

"Whatever, I'm going out." He said and moved to pull on his shoes. The three of us didn't say anything else as he got ready to leave.

Sadie only spoke after the door shut behind him, "I'm cold now."

I looked over at her and watched her tiny body shiver.

"I'll get you some nice, warm blankets, okay?"

"Okay." Her voice trembled. I stood up and grabbed the blankets from her room. I threw them in the dryer and set the time for five minutes. After the dryer beeped, I took the blankets out and brought them to Sadie. She draped them around herself and clung on tightly, enjoying the warmth. I felt her forehead and noticed she was sweating despite being cold, which meant her fever was starting to break. I was about to offer to get her something to eat again, but I realized she closed her eyes. I decided to let her sleep and laid back on the couch myself, shutting my eyes to rest for a few minutes.

-:-:-:-:-:-:-:-:-:-:-:-:-

I didn't realize I fell asleep until I was woken up by my phone buzzing nonstop. As I searched for my phone, I noticed Sadie was curled up against my side still asleep. I finally found my buzzing phone on the coffee table and grabbed it in a way that wouldn't wake Sadie. I opened it and saw I had a bunch of messages from Danny.

Dude, where are you? Why aren't you in class? Why didn't you tell me you weren't going to be in class? You're seriously gonna make me suffer through Shakespeare by myself. Are you sick? I'm not doing your half of the work. Are you okay? Paxton?

I smiled at my phone and typed a reply, My little sister had a fever, so I stayed home with her.

Danny replied within seconds, despite being in the middle of eighth period, Is she alright?

I glanced over at Sadie curled into my side and put my hand to her forehead. She felt slightly cooler which was a good sign.

Yeah, she's getting better.

Was everything alright after I left yesterday? Danny changed the subject. I thought back to walking into the house after Danny left last night. Dad was waiting for me on the couch and immediately starting yelling at me about respect and authority. I've come to the point where I tune out most of his scolding, because it seems to just be a projection of his own miserable life choices.

Nothing I couldn't handle. I replied.

Okay, well Mrs. Anderson is walking around checking our work, so I gotta go. Danny said.

I sent back a simple 'bye' and set my phone down. Since it was eighth period, school would be over soon. Penny had work right after school and Polly signed up for a free after school art club at the middle school. It would run for the next couple of weeks, so she would be walking home later.

I decided it was time to wake Sadie up, "Sadie, hey Sadie, it's time to wake up."

Her eyes slowly fluttered open and she looked at me.

"You haven't eaten anything all day, you hungry?" I asked.

"No." She replied, groggily.

"You have to eat something. How about some crackers?"

"I'm not hungry." She said.

"Well, I am, so I'm going to get myself some crackers." I stood up from the couch. I retrieved the crackers and brought them back into the living room. I ate one and then another before Sadie reached up and snagged one from my plate. I watched as she took tiny bites and slowly finished it. She ate three more and stopped. It wasn't the amount I wanted her to eat, but at least she had something in her stomach.

"I'm home!" Sidney called out as he entered the house.

"We're right here." I said and Sidney looked over at us on the couch.

"Oh." Was all he said before he took his shoes off and climbed the stairs.

I turned the tv back on for Sadie before getting up. I was finishing putting all of our clothes in the washer when a knock came from the front door.

I opened the front door and saw Danny with a pizza box in his hands.

"What are you doing here?" I asked.

"I told you I wasn't going to do your half of the work just because you missed school." He stated simply.

I looked at him in shock, "You can't just show up unannounced."

"Yeah, sorry about that, but I brought pizza." He lifted up the pizza box to emphasize his point.

"What if my dad comes home while you're here again? Did you learn nothing from last night?" I asked.

"I won't be here long. Just long enough for you to finish your part of today's assignment." Danny explained.

"Is it a lot?" I questioned. I was really happy I wouldn't have to do any work for a day, but Danny had to ruin that.

"Just half the questions for the scene and a worksheet Mrs. Anderson passed out in class." He answered.

"Okay, that doesn't seem too bad." I sighed in relief.

"Yeah, it isn't. You gonna let me in, now?" Danny pretended the pizza box was getting too heavy to hold.

"Oh, right." I mumbled and stepped aside to let him in.

"You brought pizza?" Sadie asked from the couch once she noticed the pizza box in Danny's hand.

"I did and I made it all cheese, because mushrooms are gross." Danny told Sadie.

"Mushrooms are yucky." Sadie agreed and Danny just chuckled.

"You feeling any better?" I asked Sadie.

"A little." She responded plainly and turned her attention back to the tv since her show was starting back up from commercials.

"We can work at the kitchen table since Sadie is in here." I told Danny. He nodded and followed me into the kitchen. He quickly made himself comfortable at the table and took a slice of pizza from the box.

"Would it have killed you to get half mushroom?" I asked after grabbing myself a slice of the cheese pizza.

"First, mushrooms are disgusting. Second, I brought it to you for free, so you can't complain. And, third, I get a discount at my work for one full topping pizzas only and I wasn't about to get all mushroom." Danny replied.

"Whatever, let's just start the assignment." I gave up trying to convince him that mushrooms were good.

We finished all the work within an hour and decided to eat the rest of the pizza for dinner. Polly's art club let out, so she was home and Sidney came down to eat with us. Danny clicked instantly with my siblings. He talked with Sid about some racing program on tv and he bonded with Polly over their shared hatred of mushrooms.

"Put this one down." I instructed Sadie. We decided after dinner to play a card game. Our options were limited, so we picked Uno. Sadie was feeling better, but didn't want to play by herself, so I suggested we played as a team. Sadie grabbed the blue card from my hand and placed it on the center pile. She then readjusted herself on my lap as Danny played a card.

"Change the color to green." He said as he put down a wild, draw four.

"No fair." Sidney mumbled as he drew four cards.

"I win!" Polly announced, excitedly as she placed her only card left on the pile. It was a green two.

"You just handed her the win!" Sidney yelled at Danny. I laughed along with Danny and collected the cards.

"How could I know that her last card was a green?" Danny defended himself.

"You're just supposed to know, man." Sidney muttered.

"Okay, it's getting late." I said as I lifted Sadie off my lap, "You've had a rough day, so why don't you try to get some sleep. Then, if you feel better in the morning you can try going to school."

Sadie nodded her head and made her way up the stairs. Polly and Sidney soon followed which left Danny and I alone.

"So, do you think you'll be back to school tomorrow?" Danny asked.

I looked over at him, "Yeah, Sadie seems better, so she'll probably be good to go back."

"Good, English was almost unbearable without you."

"Oh, come on, the class isn't that bad." I tried to reason.

Danny shot me a sharp look, "Fine, then I'll decide to play hooky one day and not tell you. Let me know how you like it."

I laughed at his seriousness and watched as his face slowly changed from mock anger to a smile. Both of our expressions changed though when headlights illuminated the living room around us.

"Shit, my dad's home." I whispered.

# Chapter 7

"What do you want me to do?" Danny quickly asked.

"I don't know. He can't see you after he freaked out just last night from you being here." I said. I frantically peaked through the blinds and watched as dad got out of his car slowly. He swayed with every step, which showed me that he was extremely drunk.

"I can leave through the back door or hide maybe?" Danny suggested.

I looked at him and then back outside, "Fuck."

"What? What is it?" He rushed over to stand next to me by the blinds.

"Your car is in the driveway." I stated the obvious factor we both forgot.

"Shit." Danny muttered.

"Well, hide anyway. Maybe he won't notice the car if he's too drunk." I instructed. Danny looked around the living room frantically.

"Dude, just pick somewhere." I told him.

"I don't know if you noticed this, Paxton, but your house doesn't have many good hiding spots." He hissed at me.

We both froze as the front door swung open. Dad staggered in, took his shoes off, and walked up the stairs without uttering a single word or even glancing in our general direction. We both stayed absolutely still until we heard his bedroom door slam shut.

I slowly turned around to face Danny, "Did he just?...Did that just?..."

"I guess he finally warmed up to me." Danny joked.

"Yeah, right. He was just too drunk to notice you were even here." I scoffed.

"Either way that was hilarious. You should've seen your face when he pulled up." He was laughing even harder now.

I glared at him, "You looked just as terrified."

"No, that was all you." He tried to convince me.

"Keep telling yourself that." I gave up.

Danny laughed a little more before collecting his things and putting his shoes on. We said our goodbyes at the door and I watched his car disappear from our street before closing the door.

That was such a dangerous close call, yet in that moment I never felt more alive.

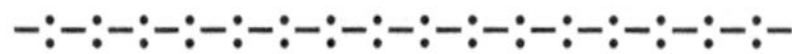

"If one more kid decides it is a good idea to throw two bowling balls down the lane at once, I'm going to punch something." I complained to Hannah as I joined her back behind the front counter.

It was Friday and I was working the closing shift at the bowling alley with Hannah. The alley was packed, because Linda decided to start having Friday night cosmic bowling. All it consisted of was flashing neon lights in replace of the normal ones and we took music requests from the costumers that we played through the stereo. It wasn't anything fancy, but Linda advertised it all throughout the city as 'new Friday fun for the whole family' and people wanted to check it out. Linda could also take the opportunity to raise the prices, because of the 'heightened experience' we were giving.

"As long as it's not me you punch, I'm cool with it." Hannah replied.

"No promises."

"How much longer until closing?" She asked.

I checked the big clock on the wall behind us, "About two more hours."

"I can't sit here and scroll through music requests for the next two hours. Can we switch jobs?" Hannah asked me. I was currently working the front where people bought games and got their shoes and Hannah was taking song requests and playing them through the speakers.

"I don't know if I want to do your job." I told her.

"Please, Paxton." She begged.

"Fine," I agreed, "Only, because you said 'please'".

"Thank you!" She bounced up from her spot and quickly pushed me away from the register. I stood by the old desk top computer we were getting the music from and looked through the notebook that people wrote their suggestions in. I chose the next one and clicked play on the computer. It was some country song and a lane with a big family at it started cheering when they heard it.

I continued selecting and playing songs for the next half an hour. People would constantly come up to the notebook and write down their requests. It wasn't a hard job, but it was boring, so I realized why Hannah didn't want it for another two hours.

"Does anyone actually suggest any good songs around here?" A voice asked me. I looked up from the computer and saw Danny standing on the other side of the counter.

"Oh, hey." I greeted.

"Hey."

"You here by yourself?" I questioned. I looked slightly behind him and didn't see any of his friends.

"No, I'm here with two of my friends, Anthony and Brian. They are over there getting our lane set up." Danny pointed to lane eight. I noticed the two boys were the same ones I've seen here before with Danny's friend group.

I nodded in recognition, "Well, the only way to get the music you want is by requesting it."

"Can I get my song bumped up on the list since I know the DJ?" Danny smirked at me.

"Sorry, no friend of employees benefits." I joked back.

"Damn, that sucks." He said as he pulled the notebook towards him and grabbed the pen. He wrote down a song and slide the paper back towards me. He started to walk away when he whipped back around.

"Oh, I forgot I was going to ask you something." He said, "Are you going to the big end of summer party at the lake? My friends and I will be there."

I stared at him for a second. Every year the high schoolers have an end of summer party down by the lake at the outskirts of the city. It's like the last big event for teenagers before it starts to get cold. Everyone is invited, but I've never gone. Penny went her freshman year of high school and I know she was planning on going again this year with Sidney, so I was planning on just staying home with the two youngest.

"Oh, I don't know." I responded.

"You totally should, it's going to be a lot of fun." Danny said.

"I wouldn't have a ride and it's too far to walk." I blurted out the first excuse I could think of.

"I can pick you up and drive you home." He immediately offered.

"Well, Penny and Sidney are going with their friends, so I have to watch Polly and Sadie." I made another excuse.

Danny leaned his arms on the counter, "How old is Polly?"

"Eleven." I replied.

"I'm sure for one night, they can stay home by themselves and be fine." He assured me.

"I'm not sure if that's the best idea."

"Come on, Paxton, live a little. Why don't you think about it and you can text me your decision in the morning?"

I thought over his preposition before nodding, "Okay."

"Great." Danny tapped the counter with his hands before pushing off and walking towards his friends.

I decided to forget about our conversation for now and flipped the song request notebook around, so I could read it. I smiled slightly when I saw the song Danny suggested was I Lived by OneRepublic.

With five minutes until closing, I shut down the computer and closed the notebook. Hannah gave the customers a closing warning and flipped the lights back on. We both stood behind the counter and collected all the shoes.

"I'm going to start collecting the trash." Hannah told me before walking off towards the lanes. I started spraying the shoes with cleaner and noticed Danny walking towards the counter with Anthony and Brian. They placed their shoes up on the counter and his two friends walked away as Danny leaned on the edge.

"Do you have a ride home?" He asked.

"No." I replied.

"Want me to drive you home?" I looked at Danny and then behind him to his two friends. They were pushing each other around playfully and laughing.

I shook my head, "No, it's a nice night out. You should go with your friends."

Danny turned over his shoulder and watched his friends shove each other before looking back at me, "It's really no trouble, I can—."

"Really, Danny, I'll be fine." I cut him off.

He looked me in the eye for a few seconds before shrugging, "Okay, just be careful."

"I will."

He walked away towards his friends before calling from over his shoulder, "Don't forget to think about tomorrow!"

He left with Anthony and Brian, leaving me alone in the bowling alley with Hannah. I finished spraying the shoes and joined Hannah by the lanes.

"I'll sweep the floors and get the balls back on their racks. Can you take the trash out? You know the back of the building freaks me out. Especially, now that the light above the door flickers." Hannah shuddered at the thought.

"Yeah." I said and grabbed the two trash bags. I took the trash out to the dumpster and when I returned Hannah was out of her uniform, ready to leave.

"You can go, I'll lock up." I told her. She nodded at me and said goodbye before walking out the door. I changed out of my own uniform and shut off all the lights. I left the building, locked the door, and started walking home.

The only thought that plagued my mind on the way home was what my answer to Danny was going to be.

-:-:-:-:-:-:-:-:-:-:-:-:-:-

"I'm going over to Marissa's house until the party. She offered to lend me a bathing suit for tonight." Penny announced the next morning after breakfast.

"Okay." I replied. I was on the couch with Sadie as she played with one of her hand-me-down stuffed animals.

"Marissa is going to drive us there and back, so tell Sidney to be ready by six. We will stop by to pick him up before we go." She said.

"Okay, I'll let him know when he wakes up." I promised.

She left the house, leaving me and Sadie alone. I still hadn't decided if I was going to go tonight. On one hand, I was nervous about leaving Polly alone to watch Sadie. She was eleven and although I've been home alone at a way younger age than that, it was different. I was the oldest and it was my responsibility to make sure my siblings were safe, because it's obvious dad won't. On the other hand, I also wanted to follow

Danny's advice and 'live a little'. I've never gone to parties or school functions before, because I've never known anyone, but now I did know someone. I knew Danny. He seemed to want me there and it was only one night out. Polly was a very smart and logical kid, she should be fine watching herself and Sadie for one night.

I looked down at Sadie playing peacefully with her stuffed animal and searched for my phone before I changed my mind. I finally found it and opened up to Danny's contact.

What time should I be ready for you to pick me up? I typed.

# Chapter 8

"I will be home before morning and if dad comes home—."

"Avoid him at all costs. Yeah, I got it, Pax." Polly said. I was explaining everything for about the tenth time just in case anything happened while I was at the party. To say Polly was getting agitated was an understatement.

"And make sure Sadie goes to bed at a reasonable time." I told her.

"Everything will be fine, Paxton." She said.

After I texted Danny that I was going earlier, I instantly regretted it. My mind went into overdrive and I couldn't stop thinking of every possible way the night could end horribly for my two youngest sisters. I would never forgive myself if anything happened to them, but Polly insisted she was old enough to take care of everything. I wasn't too convinced an eleven year old was responsible enough to stay home alone with a seven year old, but it wasn't just any eleven year old. It was

Polly. She was bright and thought everything out before taking action, so I had to believe her.

I was about to remind her of not letting Sadie mess with any of the kitchen appliances when my phone buzzed. It was Danny telling me he was in the driveway and to hurry up. I grabbed my jacket and tied my shoes before saying goodbye to Polly and Sadie. I walked outside and got into Danny's car. Once I was inside, I let out a huge breath.

"Don't get out much, do you?" He asked, lightly.

"It's just...what if something happens to them and—." I started.

"They will be fine, Paxton, I promise. You're allowed to have a normal teenage life too." Danny cut me off.

I looked over at him, "My life is the farthest thing from normal."

"Okay, maybe, but tonight I am going to make sure you experience a completely carefree and normal teenage party." Danny promised. I gave him a small smile and put on my seatbelt. He then put the car in reverse and backed out of the driveway.

We got to the lake in twenty minutes and the parking lot was packed. We eventually found an open spot and got out.

"Help me get the blankets and water." Danny told me while opening his trunk.

"You brought water to a high school party?" I asked. I might not have been to a lot of parties during high school, but I knew for a fact no one drank water at them.

"Oh, trust me, people will need these after they start puking behind the bushes past midnight." Danny laughed.

"Wow, look at you being the responsible friend." I joked.

"You know it. I'll take the blankets and one case if you take the other two." He collected the blankets and grabbed one case of water. I grabbed the other two and shut the trunk for him. We then made the slight hike down to the lake. I knew we were close when the sound of loud music and people talking got almost unbearable.

"Let's drop the water off at the drink table over there." Danny motioned to the picnic table full of alcoholic beverages. I nodded and we walked over. Most of the drinks were already opened and halfway gone which didn't surprise me since it seemed the whole school was here. We set the water cases under the table and Danny reached for the solo cups.

"It's about time you showed up." A voice greeted from behind us. Danny turned around and smiled at the two boys behind him. I recognized them as Anthony and Brian from the bowling alley yesterday.

"Hey, guys. Where's everyone else?" Danny asked.

"Kathrine was complaining about having to sit on the itchy grass, so Ava and Hudson went with her to get some blankets from the truck." One of them explained.

"Too bad they didn't wait a few minutes, because I brought blankets." Danny lifted up the blankets in his hands.

"I'm Brian and this is Anthony by the way, since Danny sucks at introducing people." The shorter of the two boys said to me.

"I'm Paxton and yeah I've noticed he isn't too good at that." I replied.

"I was getting around to it if you just gave me a second." Danny tried to defend himself.

"How do you two know each other?" Anthony asked.

"We are English partners, so he's stuck being my friend for at least a few months." Danny joked.

"He doesn't have to be your friend just because you are English partners." Brian said.

"He's right, I don't, so why am I hanging out with you again?" I joked.

"Can we all stop making fun of me, now? You were my friend first Paxton, so stop teaming up against me with my other friends." Danny pouted.

We all laughed at his expense.

"Oh good, you're here. Danny, you have to try this drink I mixed together." A boy jogged over to us. He was being followed by two girls carrying blankets.

"Hudson, last time I tried a drink you mixed I got sick." Danny said.

"Trust me this one is good." Hudson shoved the red solo cup at Danny. Danny took it and sniffed it before taking a small sip.

"Oh wow, this is actually pretty good." He complimented.

"See, told you."

"Uh, guys this is Paxton. We have the same English class and I invited him to hang out with us tonight. Paxton, this is Hudson, Kathrine, and Ava." Danny introduced me.

"Hi." I greeted. They all gave their 'hellos' with kind smiles.

We all small talked for a little bit by the drinks before Kathrine complained about having to hold the blankets, so we decided to find a place to sit by the lake. Danny shared his blanket with me and gave the other one he brought to Anthony and Brian, who I found out were brothers. Brian was a sophomore while the rest of us were seniors. I also learned that Ava, Brian, and Hudson were all on the schools tennis team and Kathrine was actually our student body president which I did not know.

Once it got dark out a few of the football players started a big bonfire. We moved our blankets closer, so we could feel the heat radiating off the flames.

It was nice around Danny's friends. They were easy to talk to and didn't ask any questions about me hanging out with them for the night. I felt like I was apart of something. They all joked around with each other and were so carefree. There was no feeling of judgement, just a contentment with life and love for each other. The feeling was the same one I noticed I was missing that night I watched them all interact at the bowling alley.

"I need more beer." Hudson announced and stumbled to get up.

"I'll come with you, so your drunk ass doesn't get hurt." Brian said and got up too before they both left towards the drink table.

"Anyone up for some late night swimming?" Kathrine asked, excitedly. The lake had a few people splashing around in it, but most people were just sitting on the side hanging out.

"I'm in." Ava said and striped herself of her shirt, revealing a bikini top underneath. Kathrine did the same and soon they were both standing in only their swimsuits.

"Anyone else coming?" Kathrine asked.

"Sure I'll go." Anthony shrugged and took off his shirt too. He came wearing his swim trunks, so he was ready to go.

"Danny? Paxton?" Ava questioned.

I shook my head 'no' at the same time Danny said, "I'll join later."

"Well, don't wait up." Kathrine said before grabbing Ava's hand and running off towards the lake. I heard them scream and giggle as their skin touched the water, Anthony following close behind.

"Your friends are cool," I told Danny, "and nice."

"Yeah, we're all really close. I've known Kathrine, Anthony, and Brian since we were kids. It's actually funny, because Anthony's parents would make him take Brian with him everywhere he went, so we used to see him as an annoying little tagalong, but as we all got older we just started seeing him as our little brother." He said.

"What about Hudson and Ava?" I asked.

"We met Hudson in middle school after him and Anthony got in a fight. They both got sent to the principals office and somehow came out as friends. Hudson then met Ava at tennis practice freshman year and had a thing for her. She never liked him back, but her and Kathrine got close after he introduced her to all of us. We've all been friends since." He explained.

"Wow, I wish we met in a cool way too. Meeting in English class isn't really a good story to tell." I said.

"Well, technically the first time we met was at your doorstep as I delivered your gross half mushroom pizza." Danny reminded me.

"Mushrooms are not gross!" I argued. Mushrooms were delicious and I would defend them forever.

"Keep telling yourself that." He laughed.

"I brought drinks for everyone!" Hudson yelled. He came back over to us with his hands full of drinks. He stumbled as he walked which told me he really didn't need anymore alcohol.

"Where did everyone go?" Brian asked.

"Swimming." Danny replied.

"More drinks for us then!" Hudson slurred. I tried not to cringe at his very evident drunk state and had to remind myself that he wasn't my dad. He was just a teenager having fun and being stupid.

Hudson started to lazily hand out the cups to Danny and Brian before trying to give me one.

"No thanks." I turned him down.

"What? Who doesn't drink at a party?" Hudson questioned and tried to hand me the cup again.

"No, really. I'm good." I tried again.

"Come on man, you haven't had one drink all night. Loosen up a bit." He nudged me. For the first time all night I felt uncomfortable. Danny's friends were very welcoming and kind people and I'm sure Hudson was too, but he was drunk right now. I know better than anyone that people aren't the same when they're drunk.

"I don't want a drink." I said, a little more forceful.

"Just one drink, man. It won't—." Hudson started.

"He said no, Hudson. Leave him alone." Danny interrupted. I let out a breath and silently thanked him.

"Okay, chill man. It was just one drink." Hudson said and plopped down on his blanket.

"He said he didn't want it, so just drop it. Paxton, can you come help me get something out of the car?" Danny asked me.

"Uh, sure." I said, shakily. I stood up and walked with Danny all the way to his car.

"Hey, I'm sorry about, Hudson. He's just had too much to drink." Danny apologized.

"It's fine. I knew people would be drinking tonight. Hell, Penny and Sidney are probably drinking wherever they are around here too. I'm just not used to being around drunk people who aren't my dad." I explained.

"Well, I can't say this for Hudson, but Kathrine is a funny drunk. She'll make you laugh harder than you've ever laughed before. Ava, though, is a clumsy drunk. She'll fall over everything and anything, so I bet you can imagine how great the two of them are drunk together." Danny laughed at past memories.

I smiled and watched him open his backseat car door. He pulled out a duffel bag and swung it over his shoulder. He then closed the door and locked the car.

I stared at him and the duffel bag in confusion, "What's that?"

Danny smirked at me and shrugged the bag off his shoulder. He threw it down on the top of his car hood before unzipping it. He then pulled out two articles of clothing that I realized were swim trunks.

He wiggled the trunks in front of my face, "We're going swimming."

# Chapter 9

"We? I think you mean you're going swimming." I replied. There was no way I was going s          w          i          m          -ming.

"Oh, come on, Paxton. I said you were going to experience a real high school party tonight and that includes actually living like a teenager." Danny said.

"I don't swim." I tried.

Danny's face softened slightly, "You don't know how to swim?"

"I mean, I know how to swim, but—."

"Great, then you're going swimming." He threw one of the swim trunks at me. It was a light blue color and the one he was still holding was maroon.

"Danny, I really don't want to." I said. Something about being in a murky lake in the dark with a bunch of people I didn't know wasn't appealing to me.

"Please, Paxton. I promise you'll have fun." He pleaded.

I looked at the swim trunks in my hand and then back at Danny, "Fine."

"Okay, good. Now go put those on." He instructed. I glanced around the parking lot and didn't see any restrooms.

"Where?" I asked.

"Find a tree." Danny shrugged at me.

"You're kidding." I could practically feel my eyes pop out of their sockets.

"Nope. You gotta become one with nature, Paxton." He chuckled and pushed me in the direction of a tree.

I groaned and hid myself behind a big tree. I quickly changed out of my pants and into the swim trunks. Danny and I had similar builds, he was just the tiniest bit taller than me, so his swimsuit fit me pretty well.

"Ready?" Danny asked when I emerged from behind the tree.

"No." I muttered, but followed Danny back towards the lake anyway.

"Took you two long enough to join us." Kathrine said as we approached the water.

"Good, we'll finally have enough for chicken. I call Anthony as my base." Ava said as she splashed Anthony with water.

"Oh, you did it now." Anthony threatened. Ava shrieked right before Anthony lunged at her and pulled her under the water.

Danny started to walk into the water, but stopped when he noticed I wasn't following.

"Come on, Paxton. The water's warm." He told me.

When I didn't move he reached his arm out. I looked at his hand and then into his eyes. They were sincere and patient. They told me he was going to stand there and wait until I went in with him. I took a deep breath and connected our hands. He tugged me forward lightly and my body followed willingly. I was soon standing right next to him and we walked deeper into the water together. The water was a comfortable temperature and I could feel the rocks beneath my toes. Danny didn't let go of my hand until we needed our arms to stay above water.

"Welcome to being a teenager, Paxton." Danny whispered in my ear.

"Danny come be my base for chicken!" Kathrine yelled. We swam over to Anthony, Kathrine, and Ava. Kathrine climbed on Danny's shoulders and Ava did the same to Anthony. I watched in amusement as they pushed and screamed, trying to knock each other off. Anthony and Ava won after Danny lost his footing.

"A and A for the win!" Ava cheered and gave Anthony a high-five.

"Let's go jump of the ledge." Kathrine suggested after resurfacing. On the side of the lake was a big rock ledge. I watched earlier as people jumped off doing cool flips and tricks. We swam over to below the edge and looked up at it. Once we were right under it, the height intimidated me. I decided I wasn't going to jump off.

"Hey, Paxton, come jump off with Ava and me." Kathrine suggested.

I instantly shook my head, "I don't really think—."

"You need to live a little, Paxton. Tonight will be a waste if I didn't get you to do anything adrenaline pumping." Danny cut me off.

"It'll be fun. We jump off every year." Kathrine added.

I looked up at the towering ledge and nodded before I could change my mind. I followed Ava and Kathrine out of the lake and climbed up to the ledge behind them. Once we got to the top, my heart started pumping. It looked scary from below, but being on the edge was scarier.

"Together on three." Kathrine said. She grabbed Ava's hand with one of her own and then mine with her other. We crept up to the edge of the ledge and looked down. Anthony and Danny were staring up at us from the water.

"I'll be right here to catch you!" Danny jokingly yelled up.

"Okay, one, two, three!" Kathrine yelled. We all jumped off together, my hand immediately strayed from her grasp. I hit the water sooner than I anticipated and felt my whole body submerged under water. My heart was pounding, but I felt alive. The loud music that was still blaring from the lakeside became muffled and the water was cool on my skin. My ears soon filled with sound once again as my head broke through the surface and I was surprised to see Danny right in front of me.

"Shit, you scared me." I swore.

"I told you I would catch you." He chuckled.

"You failed." I said.

"Yeah, you're right. I just wanted to do this." He said before coming at me and wrapping his arms around my body. He jumped up and pushed us both under the water. We became a mess of tangled up limbs and ended up getting stuck under for longer than anticipated. By the time we came back up, I was the one with my arms wrapped around Danny. I had my arms around his neck while he still had his arms around my waist. We stayed in that position for a few seconds trying to catch our breath. It was only after my breathing came back to me that I noticed our close proximity. I also noticed our faces were so close I could feel Danny's labored breaths on my nose. It was dark so I couldn't really see past Danny's face, but I could tell his eyes were scanning my face. We locked eyes for a split second before a voice pierced the air.

"Look out below!" Hudson screamed from the top of the ledge before running forwards and cannon balling into the lake.

Danny and I got splashed by the wave Hudson created and I took the opportunity to pull myself away from him.

"Hudson, I take my eyes off you for two seconds and you do this. You are too drunk to be swimming." Brian shouted from the lakeside.

"I'm only slightly buzzed." Hudson tried to argue, but the slur in his voice did him no favors.

"It's about time we get out anyway." Danny announced to all his friends. Everyone listened to him and swam back to the lakeshore. We all sat around to dry off as Anthony and Brian went to get us waters. We talked for about another hour as people around us slowly started leaving. Ava made Hudson drink two full water bottles to try and sober him up a little, but it didn't really work.

"I have to get Paxton home, so I'll talk to you guys later." Danny announced a little after one in the morning.

"It was nice meeting you, Paxton." Kathrine said.

"You too." I replied. Everyone else said their own goodbyes before Danny and I left.

We were silent as we made our way through the woods back to the parking lot. It wouldn't have been ideal to talk anyway though, because at almost every tree we passed couples were making out. I paid them no mind until we passed two people and one of them looked familiar. I tilted my head to see and saw no other then Sidney sucking off some girls face.

"Fuck." I swore before I could stop myself. Danny stopped walking and the two people making out quickly ceased to look over at us. I made eye contact with Sidney and even though it was dark I knew he was blushing.

"Hey, Paxton." He said, awkwardly.

"Um, hi." I replied. I wasn't mad at my little brother for making out with some girl at a party. I was just caught off guard and couldn't keep my mouth shut long enough to just keep walking.

"This is, uh, Riley. Riley, this is my brother Paxton." Sid introduced us.

"Oh, hi. Nice to meet you." She said, confidently. She clearly wasn't embarrassed about the whole situation.

"Okay, we are going to be leaving now." Danny announced from the side and grabbed my arm to pull me away.

He kept his hold on my arm all the way to the car.

"Can I have my arm back?" I asked once we stopped at the car.

"Oh, yeah sorry." He dropped my arm from his grasp.

"Do you want me to give you back your swim trunks?"

"No, you can just wear them home and bring them to school on Monday." Danny answered.

I nodded as he unlocked his car. We put the blankets in his trunk and took our respective seats. He started the ignition and pulled out of the half empty parking lot.

"Your face was priceless." Danny busted out laughing once we got on the road.

"Oh, shut up. I was just caught off guard." I muttered.

"Oh, trust me, I put that together. You looked like you caught them having sex." He laughed.

"I just didn't know my brother was dating anyone." I said. I wasn't even sure if they were dating. Tonight could've been a one time hookup that we interrupted. I tried not to think about that though, because I couldn't handle the thought of my little brother getting it on at fourteen. I always forget my siblings are growing up.

"Well, I can definitely say I accomplished giving you a normal teenage party experience. Maybe, a little too much of the experience." Danny continued to laugh.

"Just shut up."

Danny continued to joke about Sidney until we pulled onto my street. I pretended he was just trying to pick on me and be annoying, but I knew the real reason. He didn't want to leave any silence for us to talk about what happened at the lake.

"Well, the house is still standing. That's a good sign." I said as we pulled up to my house.

"I told you everything would be fine." Danny said.

"Thanks for taking me tonight. I actually had a lot of fun." I admitted to Danny.

"Then I did my job well." He chuckled.

"See you at school on Monday." I said as I got out.

"Bye."

I walked up to the door and stepped inside. I watched out the window as Danny left only after I shut the door completely. All the lights were off downstairs, which told me Sadie and Polly were in their room. I took my shoes off and crept up the stairs quietly. I pushed open their door and saw both of them sound asleep in their bunk bed. I smiled at them before retreating and going into my room. I changed out of Danny's swim trunks and put them over my bed rest to dry completely.

I couldn't help but smile as I relived the night over and over again in my head. It was the most fun I've had in a long time and I had Danny to thank for that. He persuaded me to leave the house and he was the one who made me live carefree for the night. The moment with Danny in the lake left me slightly confused, but I figured we would talk about it when we were both ready to.

My main focus was Sidney. Once I had the time to let the situation with Sid sink in, I couldn't help but laugh. I was going to tease him about catching him with that girl, Riley, for the rest of his life.

# Chapter 10

I walked into computer class Monday morning expecting to fool around on my desktop while the teacher talked about our next assignment. I didn't expect a girl to drop her book bag down beside mine and sit at the computer right next t                                                                    o me.

"Hey, Paxton." The girl greeted me.

I looked over, confused, but grinned when I realized who it was, "Oh, hey, Ava. I didn't know you were in this class."

"Yeah, I always sit by myself at that computer over there, but now that we know each other I figured we could sit together." She pointed to a different computer across the classroom.

"Do you know how photoshop works?" I asked.

"I know the basics." She shrugged.

"Then as long as you help me figure it out, you can sit next to me." I said.

She giggled, "Fair trade."

We spent the rest of class making small talk as Ava worked on the assignment and I played computer games. I worked on the assignment for the first half of class, but soon got bored and quit.

"Do you have lunch next period?" Ava asked as she saved her work and shut off her computer.

"Yeah, I do." I replied. I normally just did class work at a table by myself during lunch to make sitting alone a little more bearable.

"You should sit with my friends and me. It's just everyone you met on Saturday at the lake. Oh, but you probably have your own friends you sit with, duh."

"No, I'd love to sit with you guys. As long as it's okay with everyone." I accepted her offer.

"Paxton, everyone loved hanging out with you on Saturday. They'll be cool with it." She said.

"Okay." We had to wait a few minutes before the bell rang. We then walked out of the classroom and towards the cafeteria. As we got closer, the loud chatter of students and the smell of gross school lunches filled my senses. Ava led me to a table on the side where Kathrine and Hudson were sitting.

"Hi, Ava. Oh, hi, Paxton." Kathrine greeted.

"Paxton's in my computer class, so I invited him to sit with us at lunch." Ava explained.

"Cool." Hudson said as he took a big bite out of his sandwich.

"You can sit next to me." Ava said as she set her stuff down. She took the seat to the left of Kathrine, so I took the one left of her.

Danny and the brothers then came walking towards the table. Anthony and Brian sat down next to each other beside Hudson. Danny then took the seat next to Anthony, across from me.

"Hey, Paxton." Danny greeted me as he sat down.

"Hey." I replied.

"We have the same computer class before this period and I invited him to sit with us." Ava explained once again. The three just nodded in understanding and started digging into their lunches.

"Oh, I have your swim trunks." I said to Danny and pulled the light blue shorts out of my book bag.

"Thanks." He said as he grabbed them from my hands and put the trunks in his own book bag.

The group of friends started making conservation with one another, but I couldn't find myself able to participate. I also didn't bring a lunch today, because I'm normally not hungry enough for it. I ended up pulling out my science book and notebook to get a head start on my vocabulary definitions.

"Do you not have a lunch?" Danny asked after I pulled out my schoolwork.

"No, I don't usually bring one." I answered.

"Don't you get hungry?" Brian asked.

"No, not really." I responded.

"That's crazy, I'm always hungry." Hudson chimed in.

"We know." Kathrine and Ava said simultaneously.

"I have an extra granola bar in my bag if you want it." Kathrine offered.

"No, it's okay. I'm really not that hungry."

"Just take it anyway. Maybe you'll get hungry in one of your other classes, today." She handed me the granola bar.

I took it slowly, "Thanks."

"Of course. Hey, did anyone do Mrs. Drury's homework from last week?"

They continued talking for the rest of lunch and I joined in occasionally. It was nice having other people to sit with at lunch, but it still amazed me how easily they all just seemed to fit with each other. Each person had a place in their friend group and they just made sense as friends. I felt like I was kind of intruding on their friendship, despite how nice and inclusive they all were. I guess I just wasn't used to having people to interact with during school hours.

-:-:-:-:-:-:-:-:-:-:-:-:-:-:-:-

"I'm going to Drew's house for a little bit. I'll probably eat dinner over there, so don't wait for me." Sidney said as he tied his shoes on. I was on the couch attempting to do some of my homework, but I didn't have the motivation.

"Are you sure you're not just going to Riley's?" I joked. Ever since I caught Sid with that girl at the lake party, I teased him about it. I even pretended I wanted to sit him down and give him 'the talk', but he was quick to assure me that he knew all about it and how to be safe.

"Can you just let that go?" He asked annoyed, but I could see a light blush spread across his cheeks.

"Never." I replied.

"Bye."

"Have fun." I said before he shut the door.

I decided to give up on my homework and checked the time. It was getting close to dinner, so I got up to make my way into the kitchen. We didn't have much of anything that I could make, so I figured it would be a good idea to order.

"Girls! Do you want to order pizza or Chinese food?" I yelled up the stairs.

"Pizza!" I received two replies from Polly and Sadie. Penny was at work, so it would just be the three of us tonight.

I dialed the pizza place with the cheapest prices just like always and waited for someone to pick up.

"Yes, I would like one large half cheese, half mushroom pizza, please." I ordered. The person on the other line took all my information before hanging up.

I went back to the couch and decided to officially give up on my homework for the night. Instead, I collected all my weekly payments from work and did the math in my head. I had to use about half for groceries this week, but the rest I saved for the bills at the end of the month. I just finished rolling up the money and tying it with a rubber band when someone knocked on the front door. I grabbed a twenty from the grocery stack and answered the door.

"Of course you're working today." I said as I was met with Danny in his work shirt and hat.

"Of course you order your gross mushroom pizza the day I'm working." He answered back.

"I'm going to make you like mushrooms even if it's the last thing I do." I handed him the twenty dollar bill.

"Yeah, good luck with that." He pulled the pizza out of the warming bag and handed it over to me. He then made change for the twenty and took the two dollar tip I gave him.

"You better do your half of the Macbeth questions for tomorrow and don't forget we have a quiz over the first four scenes." Danny reminded while closing up the warming bag.

"Do I have to? It's so boring." I said.

"Yes. I have to, so you do too. When we are both not working sometime we should do them together, so it's not as bad." He answered.

"Okay, I'm holding you to that." I responded.

We said our 'goodbyes' and I brought the large pizza to the kitchen table. I called Polly and Sadie down to eat and we dug in.

"Then at recess, we played on the monkey bars. We raced across them to see who could go faster and I w—." Sadie was telling us a story when the front door slammed open.

Dad staggered into the kitchen and took in the scene of us eating the pizza.

"Want some pizza, daddy?" Sadie asked.

"No, cupcake. I need cash for poker tonight at Stevie's." He first answered Sadie, but the second part was directed at me.

"You aren't even good at poker." I said.

"You have no idea what I'm good at and I'm your father, so give me some cash. Fifty bucks, that's it." I could hear his angry side starting to surface.

"I don't have any extra cash to give you. If you want to play poker, get your own betting money." I stood my ground. I needed all the money I had for bills and groceries, so there was no way I was going to give him any.

"Fine, I tried asking politely, but I guess I'm just going to have to take it." Dad said before turning around and heading back into the living room. I looked at where he stood confused for a moment before realization dawned on me. The rustling of papers on the coffee table confirmed my suspicion.

I jumped out of my seat and ran into the living room, "No, you can't take that. That's my money I earned on my own."

Dad was fumbling with the rubber band wrapped around my wad of cash when I entered the room. I forgot to put it away after the pizza was delivered.

"I just need fifty bucks and then I'll bring home way more than that." He continued to fumble with the rubber band.

"No, you'll just lose it all. Give me my money back!" I tried to reason with him, but I soon realized he was too drunk to rationalize with.

Before he could get any further, I lunged towards him and tried grabbing the money from his hands. He tugged back with such a force that I stumbled forward. I caught myself before I could fall over and refused to let go of the money.

"Boy, if you don't let go right now!" He yelled.

"I'm not letting you take my hard earned money for a poker game with your drinking buddies!" I screamed right back.

"I am your father which means any money you make is mine if I want it." He argued.

"I make money to keep this family afloat, not so you can just take it whenever you please."

His eyes turned dark after I said that which caused me to loosen my grip ever so slightly. He noticed this and yanked the money in his direction. I was still holding on a little, so the force of the grab pulled me forward. I crashed into dad and we were both sent tumbling to the floor.

"You little piece of shit!" Dad screamed. I quickly sat up and scanned the room. First, I saw that Polly and Sadie were standing in the doorway from the kitchen to the living room. They looked frightened which I understood, because this is the first time an argument with dad got physical. He didn't hit me or anything, but he tossed me around just to get what he wanted. Second, I noticed the wad of cash near the couch on the ground. The process of us falling must have cause dad to drop the money. I scrambled to get up, but came crashing back down to the floor with a thud after dad pulled my foot out from under me.

The wind was knocked out of me, but I quickly regained my composure to yell out, "Polly get the money and run to your room!"

I watched as Polly quickly dashed towards the couch and picked up the money. She managed to get past us towards the stairs and was in her room all before dad even had the chance to stand up.

"You bastards." Dad growled once he finally got himself standing.

"She isn't going to come out of her room until you are gone and I tell her too, so there is no way for you to get that money. I suggest you go and leave us alone for the rest of the night" I said.

"Your better remember who you're talking to, boy." Dad threatened, but left the house anyway. I let out a breath once his car was out of the driveway and riding down the street.

I turned around and took in the living room. My school papers were all over the floor, table, and couch. It looked like a wind storm blew through the house.

"Pax?" A small voice piped up from the corner. I whipped my head towards little Sadie still standing in the doorway. She looked terrified and had tears in her eyes. I knelt on the ground and opened my arms. She instantly ran over and wrapped herself around me. I sat down completely and let her sit in my lap. I rubbed her back soothingly and felt her shiver from fear in my arms.

"Shhh, it's okay. It's okay, Sadie. He's gone, Sadie. Everything's okay now."

# Chapter 11

I reached my hand into my book bag and gripped the wad of cash stored at the bottom. I let out a breath once I felt that it was still there. Carrying my money around in my book bag caused me to worry constantly, but I would rather have it with me than at home for my father to find. Especially, after the previous night.

Danny threw his book bag down at the desk beside me and took his seat. I quickly removed my hand from my bag and zipped it up.

"Hey." He greeted.

"Hi."

"Ready for the quiz?" He asked.

"Shit, I completely forgot." I groaned and rubbed my hands down my face.

"I literally reminded you just last night. Did the mushrooms on your pizza make you lose your memory?" Danny laughed, but I couldn't laugh with him.

"I'm going to fail miserably." I muttered.

"Hey, you read the scenes and answered the questions, so just try to go off what you remember. I'm sure you'll be fine." He tried to make me feel better.

The bell rang before I could reply and Mrs. Anderson started to pass out the quiz sheets. She slid one on my desk and I wrote my name on the top. I then read the first question and groaned, because I knew it was just going to get worse.

"Now that all the quizzes are turned in, you may talk quietly for the rest of the period. Now would be a good time for you get a head start on reading your next scenes." Mrs. Anderson said once the last quiz was handed in.

The classroom immediately erupted into chatter from all the different students.

"Do you work tonight?" Danny asked me.

"No, why?" I replied.

"Great, I don't either, so want to work on the assignment tonight at your place?"

At the mention of my house, I shuddered. After last night, bringing Danny over to the house was the worst idea ever.

"I can't do my house." I said.

"Oh, okay." Danny looked at me confused, but didn't say anything, "We can work at my place."

I thought his offer over. Penny wasn't working tonight and she could manage dinner and watching everyone. Plus, after last night I could use a few hours away from my house.

"Would it be okay with your parents and everything?" I asked.

"Yeah, totally. No one will be home until around dinner time anyway." Danny said.

"Okay."

We waited for the bell to ring and once it did we left the classroom with all the other students. On our way to the parking lot, I texted Penny saying I was going to a friends house to work on homework and that I would be home sometime later. Danny led me to his car and I climbed in the passengers seat as he got in the drivers side. He backed out of the spot and made his way onto the street. I noticed we were driving the opposite way of my house and into the nicer side of the city. By the time we pulled into a driveway, the houses had turned from small and close together to slightly bigger and farther apart. Each house had a nice size lawn and clean, not chipped house paint.

When I stepped out of the car, I realized how quiet the surroundings were. All that can be heard outside of my house are cars and highway traffic, but here the sounds that stood out were the birds chirping and one of Danny's neighbors mowing their grass.

I followed Danny up to the front door and watched him unlock it. The inside of his house felt cozy and smelled strongly of lavender.

"Your house is really nice." I observed.

"It's nothing fancy, just home." He replied and took off his shoes. I pulled my shoes off also and followed Danny into his living room. The room had two big, plush couches with a coffee table and a large screen television.

"We can work in here or my room." Danny gave me the choices.

"Whatever you want." I shrugged.

"My room has a desk, so let's work up there."

Danny walked past me back out of the living room and towards the staircase. I followed close behind him and kept my eyes glued to the wall beside the stairs all the way up. They were lined with family pictures. The first three were of individual children and looked to be school photos. There was one of Danny and the other two were of girls that looked like the same person. Next, was one of all three of them posed together and smiling at the camera. The next one had two older people in it, so I assumed they were Danny's parents. The last one had all five of them with a dog smiling at the camera.

Danny noticed me looking and stopped walking, "That's my two step-sisters, Jade and Amber. They're identical twins. Then, that's my mom and step-dad."

"Who's that?" I asked, pointing to the dog.

"That's Coconut. He was the twin's old dog that died a few months ago." Danny explained.

I nodded and followed Danny up the rest of the stairs. We walked into the first room on the left and I had to hold back my surprise. Danny's room wasn't how I expected it to look. I expected a slightly messy room with a bunch of different interests and hobbies hung on the walls like a typical teenage boys room. Instead, his room was very clean and everything matched the color theme of green, black, and gray.

"My mom wanted to try interior decorating a few years ago and redid our entire house." Danny said after he noticed me looking.

"It's nice."

"Well, make yourself comfortable and I call not reading first." Danny said.

"That's not fair, but fine." I replied and took a seat at his desk chair. Danny pulled up another chair next to me and pulled out his materials. I grabbed my book and worksheets and set them out on the desktop. I then started reading the beginning of the scene. We worked for about thirty minutes before we got stuck.

"I don't understand what the hell that means." I complained.

"I don't either, so I say we write down something random." Danny suggested.

I agreed and we wrote down our best guess. We had to do that for the next three questions also and I was getting annoyed.

"Someone needs to go back in time and inform Shakespeare of how we talk today, so he can write the correct way." I said.

"I agree. Hey, do you have an extra sheet of paper? I'm running low."

"Yeah, I have some in my other folder." I said. I reached over to my book bag and yanked out one of my folders. In the process, my bundle of money flew out of the bag and rolled across the floor.

"Is that—?" Danny began.

"It's nothing." I hurriedly said.

"It doesn't look like nothing." Danny got up to go investigate the same time I did, but he beat me to the cash. He held it up and glanced at the number amounts.

"Can you give me my money back?" I asked, impatiently.

"Why are you carrying around this much money?" Danny ignored me.

"It's nothing, just give it back." I reached for it, but he pulled it away.

"There has to be like four hundred dollars here." He observed.

"Danny, I'm serious, give it back." I was starting to get angry.

"Not until you tell me why you are carrying around all this money in your book bag." He said, seriously.

"I don't need to explain myself to you."

"Yes, you do if you want to get your money back."

I took a deep breath before speaking again, "Danny, please just give me my money back."

Danny looked from the money in his hand and then back at me, "Not until you tell me why it's in your book bag."

"You are being so unreasonable! Why does it matter to you that I carry my money around with me?" I was beyond frustrated.

"Because it's not normal to have this much money on you unless something is wrong." He said.

"Well, I'm not normal am I? I'm not normal, because I have to hide my hard earned money in my book bag all the time, so I know for a fact that there is no way my dad can find it and steal it from me. I'm not normal, because I have to constantly make sure I'll have enough money by the end of the week to buy groceries for my four siblings and by the end of the month, so I can come home to a house that has running water and electricity. I have my money in my book bag, because I don't have the luxury to be normal, Danny!" My chest heaved up and down after I stopped talking, because my speech took all of my air.

Danny's face softened and his eyes opened wide.

He took a few steps towards me before speaking, "I'm sorry, Paxton, I didn't know."

I sighed, "No, I'm sorry. I didn't mean to snap at you. It's just after last night, I'm on edge."

"What happened last night?" Danny's eyes turned curious and I was confused for a second before I realized what I just said.

"Never mind, I didn't mean to say that." I tried.

"No, tell me what happened last night. Was it something with your father?" He guessed.

I looked down at my feet and nodded once. Danny took a few more steps until he was right in front of me. He was close enough that his feet were now also in my view as I continued to stare at the floor. He grabbed my one hand and flipped it over. Then, he gently placed my bundle of cash into my palm. I gripped onto the money tightly, afraid to let it go.

"Is what happened last night the reason you forgot about the English quiz today?" Danny tried a different approach.

"Yeah." I played with the money in my hands.

"Did your dad come home drunk?" He asked.

I nodded my head, because I suddenly felt too exhausted to talk.

"Did he yell at you?"

I nodded again.

"So it was like it always is when he comes home?" Danny asked. He was trying to be gentle, but I could tell he was confused. It wasn't like me to break down like this just because dad yelled at me. I was used to his drunk screaming by now, because he has done it my entire life.

"Not exactly." I mumbled.

"What do you mean? What happened?" Danny's voice was growing worried.

I didn't answer, so Danny guessed.

"Did he hit you?"

I involuntarily winced at his assumption which was a mistake.

"He hit you, Paxton? Where? How many times? You told me he was just an angry drunk, not physical." His voice was turning hard.

"Look at me, Paxton." Danny demanded. I took a breath and slowly made eye contact with Danny. He was so close to me that our tiny height difference was very evident and I felt like he was towering over me.

"Tell me what happened." He instructed calmly, but I knew he wouldn't take 'no' for an answer.

"He didn't hit me. Not exactly, at least. I was eating dinner with Polly and Sadie when he came home. He walked into the kitchen asking for fifty bucks for a poker game. I told him I didn't have any extra to give him and he got mad. I was counting my money earlier in the living room and forgot to put it away after you dropped the pizza off. My dad saw it and tried to take it. I tried to grab it out of his hands, but he wouldn't let go. We ended up both wrestling each other to the ground for it and the cash flew across the room. He pulled my leg out from under me when I tried to get it." I told the story.

"He has never gotten physical like that before?" Danny asked.

"No, and it's not that he really hurt me, but he showed that he could if he wanted to. I'm just worried it won't be long before he completely snaps." I shared my true thoughts.

"So, that's why you're carrying that around everywhere." He pointed to the money in my hands.

"Yeah, but that's not even the worst part. After he left, I saw Sadie standing in the kitchen doorway. She was terrified and it took an hour to calm her down enough to send her to bed. She's only seven and I don't even want to think about my dad harming her. I can't even imagine any of my siblings getting hurt by my dad. Oh no, if he's home right now and since I'm not there Penny has to face him or if Sid tries to step in—."

"Calm down, Paxton." Danny grabbed my arms.

"You don't understand, Danny. They see me as their strong, unbreakable older brother. I have to be there for them and keep everything together." I said.

"You can't hold everything in forever. You'll end up blowing up at every semi-stressful moment." He told me.

"Too late for that." I chuckled, slightly.

Danny chuckled too, "I'm glad you talked to me about it. I'm here for you."

I glanced down at the money in my hands and noticed Danny was still holding onto my arms. I looked back up at him and saw he was already staring back at me. My stomach did a funny flip, but it wasn't uncomfortable. My mind flashed back to the lake and I realized we haven't talked about what happened yet. Now, we were in the same situation and neither of our eyes broke contact.

Danny slowly slid his hands up my arms and rested them on my shoulders. His touch was light like a feather. It felt almost nonexistent, but electric at the same time. I could've sworn Danny began to move his head closer to my own, but I'll never know for sure, because a knock came from the door.

# Chapter 12

"Honey, dinner will be ready in—oh, hello." A female voice spoke from the doorway.

Danny pulled away from me quickly and turned to face the woman. I took a step back and hid my money behind my back.

"Mom, you're home early." Danny said.

"Yeah, Roger is picking the twins up from gymnastics tonight instead of me, so I came home to start dinner." She said.

"Um, well, this is Paxton. He's a friend from school." Danny introduced us.

"It's very nice to meet you, Paxton. Will you be staying for dinner?" Danny's mom asked, kindly.

"Oh, no thanks. I have to go home for dinner." I declined.

"Okay then. Dinner will be ready in about twenty minutes, honey."

"Okay, mom." Danny said.

Danny's mom smiled at us before turning to leave. Once I could hear her footsteps going down the stairs, I crossed the room and shoved my money into my book bag. I then collected all my papers and zipped it up.

"You don't have to leave, yet. You can stay until dinner is ready." Danny said once he noticed me packing up.

"I think it's best if I just leave." I told him.

"Okay, I'll drive you home."

"It's fine, I can walk." I said.

Danny looked at me in disbelief, "Are you crazy? We live on opposite sides of the city."

"I'll be fine. I need to clear my head anyway." I swung my book bag over my shoulder.

"Clear your head in my car. There's no way I'm letting you walk all the way home." He slid past me and left his room.

By the time I followed him down the stairs, he already had his keys and was putting his shoes on. I gave in and put my shoes on too. We left the house and climbed into Danny's car.

"If you ever find yourself in trouble with your dad—." Danny started to talk after about five minutes of driving.

"I'm clearing my head, remember?" I cut him off. I wasn't in the mood to talk about my dad anymore with Danny. I needed a break.

"Right." Danny sighed. We didn't talk for the rest of the drive.

"See you at school, tomorrow?" Danny asked as I got out.

"Yeah." I said simply and shut the door.

I made my way inside and despite my coldness to Danny, he didn't reverse out of the driveway until I shut the front door.

"Pax?" Penny called out from the kitchen.

"Yeah, it's me." I said and kicked my shoes off. I walked into the kitchen and saw all my siblings eating pasta.

"We didn't know when you would be home." Penny said. She sounded slightly guilty.

"It's okay, you didn't have to wait for me." I said and grabbed a plate. I filled it up with pasta noodles from the pot and sat down with my siblings.

"So, you got friends now?" Sidney asked me with a smirk.

"Shut up, we hang out mostly just for school." I answered.

"I think it's great. Going from home to school to work everyday can't be good for you." Penny piped up.

"Just don't go asking me to babysit these two all the time now that you have friends." Sidney pointed to Polly and Sadie.

"Hey, we don't need a babysitter anymore. We were fine last weekend, weren't we?" Polly argued.

"I guess." Sid said.

"I can't believe my little sisters are starting to grow up." Penny cooed.

"I'm only seven!" Sadie spoke up.

"And you better stay that age forever. Promise me you won't get any bigger than you already are." I ruffled Sadie's hair.

Getting older just made everything more difficult. I wouldn't even hesitate if I had the chance to be Sadie's age again.

"Can I really do that?" Sadie asked, curiously.

"No, he was kidding." Sidney stated.

"Oh."

"Don't listen to Sid. I say you try to be a kid for as long as you can, okay?" I told the seven year old next to me.

"Okay! I like being a kid." She said and shoved more pasta into her mouth.

"Has dad been home yet, today?" I asked.

"No, but Kristi from work texted me he came to the restaurant looking for me." Penny said.

"What? Has he ever done that before?" I questioned.

She shook her head, "No, I didn't even think he knew where I worked."

"Did she say what he wanted?"

"Just wanted to see me." Penny shrugged.

"He knows that Pax is fed up with him, so he's probably trying to get to you for cash." Sidney said.

"Really?" Penny asked.

"Yeah, I mean why else would he come to your work place?" Sid answered.

"Well, he's mistaken if he thinks I'm giving him anything." She scoffed.

"He doesn't deserve anything from us anyway." I said with a slight edge in my voice.

We continued to eat our pasta as Sadie shared stories about her day. I only half-listened, because I was concerned about dad. He went to Penny's work and who knows how he would've acted if she was actually there. He seemed to be getting extra desperate for cash lately and I was worried.

-:-:-:-:-:-:-:-:-:-:-:-:-:-:-:-:-

"You have to use the blending tool around the edges." Ava explained.

We were in computer class and I was failing at photoshop.

"Why? I think it looks good like that." I said.

"You can't make it look like you just cut and pasted a picture onto a background." She told me.

"But that's exactly what I did."

"Yes, but the goal is that people won't be able to tell you did. Here, let me show you." She reached over and took my computer mouse from me.

I sat back and watched her easily blend out the edges of my horribly cut out picture.

"Five minutes until bell." Our teacher warned us.

"There, now save that, so you don't have to start all over." Ava moved back to her own computer. I clicked the save button and powered off my computer. Ava did the same and put on her book bag.

"Do you have a lunch, today?" She asked me.

I shook my head, "No."

I've been sitting with Danny and his friends at lunch since Ava invited me the first time. They have all been really kind towards me and seem to be letting me into their friend group more.

"Kathrine is gonna kill you. You promised her you would bring one, today." Ava warned me.

"No, I said I couldn't promise her anything." I clarified.

"Well, she sees that as a promise. Here, I'll give you an orange from my lunch, so you can avoid her wrath." Ava reached into her book bag and pulled out an orange.

"This doesn't really count as a lunch." I took the orange hesitantly.

"Kathrine will see it as taking baby steps, so you'll be fine."

The bell rang, so Ava and I walked to the cafeteria. Hudson and Kathrine were already seated when we arrived. I took a seat next to Ava as she sat next to Kathrine.

"How'd your French test go, Hudson?" Ava asked.

"I don't want to talk about it. I just don't get why we have to learn a foreign language anyway." Hudson complained.

"It's good to be able to communicate with others, plus the school wants to be able to say we got a well-rounded education." Ava replied.

"Hey." Danny greeted the table as he approached with Anthony and Brian.

"You take French, right?" Hudson asked Danny.

"No, I take Spanish." Danny answered.

"Do you all take Spanish?" Hudson asked the table.

We all nodded at him.

"Why did I sign up for French?" He groaned and dramatically put his head on the table. Brian rubbed his back soothingly.

"I think it's time for, Paxton, to show us all his amazing lunch I'm sure he brought today." Kathrine suddenly clapped her hands together.

Everyone looked at me expectedly and I gulped. I then slowly placed the orange Ava gave me on the table.

"That's it?" Kathrine asked.

"Yep." I replied.

"Oh, I can't believe you don't eat lunch. It's really not good for you." Kathrine scolded.

"You're such a mom." Hudson said.

"No, I'm just the responsible one." She responded.

"Anyway, are we going to all hang out this weekend?" Anthony asked.

Everyone responded 'yes' while I stayed quiet.

"Which house?" Hudson then asked.

"I say Ava's." Brian suggested.

"No, I can't have anyone over this weekend, because my grandparents are in town." Ava said.

"Well, our house is in the process of being painted, so we can't host." Anthony explained.

"I can't have anyone over, either." Kathrine said.

"Why not?" Hudson asked.

"Because my dad is still mad about the fireplace incident from the last time you all came over." She shared.

"That was one of the best nights of my life." Hudson laughed and high-fived Brian.

"Not for me." Kathrine muttered.

"We can hang at my place." Danny offered.

"Okay, great. Glad that's settled." Brian said.

"Are you coming, Paxton?" Ava asked me.

"Oh, um, I don't know if I'll be available." I answered. I was slightly taken-aback. I have only been spending time with Danny's friends for about a week, so to be invited to one of their out of school hangouts surprised me.

"Do you work on Saturday?" Danny questioned.

"Yeah, from ten to four."

"Are you busy after?" He then asked.

"Well, no, but—."

"Great, then you can come." He cut in.

"But, Danny—." I tried again.

"You're coming, Paxton."

"Right." I mumbled.

Hudson started in on another conversation, so I looked over at Danny. He was staring back at me with a soft expression. He gave me a small nod which told me he was still keeping his promise from the lake that he would give me a real high school experience.

I thought back to the lake and then to our moment in his room. We have yet to acknowledge any of it and I didn't even know how to bring it up. I silently came to the realization that I felt a strong connection to Danny, but I didn't know what it was exactly. Our connection as friends was definitely present, but I couldn't tell if it went farther than that. I have never had close relationships of any kind to anyone outside of my siblings and what I felt with Danny was obviously different than with my siblings. I wasn't close enough yet to the rest of his friends to know if the feeling I had was the same one I got hanging out with them too or if it was bigger. I didn't want to blow our relationship out of proportion, especially when we just recently became friends and I wasn't even certain on my feelings. The last thing I needed was to give Danny the wrong idea and lose the one friend I've ever truly had.

I looked away from Danny and focused on peeling my orange.

# Chapter 13

"I'm sorry ma'am, but I can't give you a refund after you already bowled." I said to the middle aged woman on the other side of the counter.

"This is outrageous. Our lane had so many problems that we constantly had to wait to be fixed. I shouldn't have to pay for bad service." She complained.

"I'm really sorry, but there is nothing I can do." I told her calmly.

"I would like to speak to your manger." She crossed her arms.

"Of course, I'll be right back." I left the grumpy lady at the counter and knocked on Linda's office door.

"Come in!" She called.

"There's a lady demanding a full refund for her games." I explained the situation.

"Did you tell her we don't give refunds?" She asked.

"Yes, but she won't take no for an answer and has asked to see you."

Linda put down her pen and took a deep breath before standing up.

"Wish me luck." She said as she left the office and made her way towards the front counter.

"Good luck." I called out.

I checked the clock on the wall and noticed I only had fifteen more minutes until the end of my shift. I was about to head over to the shoe area when my phone buzzed. I checked it and saw a text from Danny.

Hey, I'm on my way to the bowling alley now to pick you up after your shift.

I stared confused at my phone and typed back, Why?

I got a reply within seconds, Because we are hanging out at my house tonight, remember?

I told Danny earlier that I would come to his house after my shift, but that I might be a little late since I had to walk. The distance from the bowling alley to his house was shorter than the distance between my house and his, but it would still take about twenty minutes walking.

I can walk. I typed out.

I'm sure you can, but I'm already getting in my car and don't want my trip from my room to the driveway to be a waste. See you in fifteen. Danny texted.

I responded with a simple 'okay' and put my phone back in my pocket.

"Hey, Paxton, how has your shift been today?" Hannah asked, walking up to me. She was taking over for me after my shift.

"Busy." I replied.

"Well you will be free in ten minutes. I have to go get changed." She said and went in the direction of the locker room.

I spent the rest of my shift cleaning shoes and clocked out. I changed out of my uniform shirt and grabbed my book bag from my locker. I then said my goodbyes to Linda and Hannah before heading to the parking lot. I spotted Danny's car a few rows away and got in.

"Hey." He greeted.

"Hi."

"How was work?" He asked.

"Busy." I answered.

"Well, we are going to have a chill evening, so you can relax and have some fun for once." Danny pulled out of the parking lot.

"I have fun." I argued.

"Yeah, when you hang out with me." He retaliated.

"Okay, whatever." I let him win and leaned my head back on the seat rest.

We got to Danny's house in a few minutes and I noticed the driveway was void of cars.

"Where is everyone?" I asked.

"I texted them before we left the bowling alley, so they should be here soon and my mom and step-dad are with Jade and Amber at a gymnastics meet." Danny explained.

We got out of the car and made our way inside the house. Danny plopped down on the side of one couch and I followed by sitting on the same couch, but on the opposite end.

"I'm going to put in some pizza rolls, because Hudson and Anthony will act like rabid animals if they don't have food." Danny said and got up. He disappeared into the kitchen and I analyzed the living room.

There was a big screen television hung above a beautiful, brick fireplace. Pictures hung on the walls in here just like along the stairs. These pictures were less professional and consisted of baby pictures and Danny's step-sisters in their gymnastic leotards. There was even one from when Danny was younger in a soccer uniform.

"Okay, the pizza rolls are in the oven." Danny announced as he came back into the living room.

"You played soccer?" I asked and pointed to the picture of him. He couldn't have been any older than ten.

"Yeah my dad made me play when I was little. I was never good at it though." He said.

I was about to respond when the front door opened.

"Is that pizza rolls I smell?" Hudson's voice yelled throughout the house.

"They aren't done yet, but yes." Danny laughed as Hudson entered the living room with Ava and Kathrine.

"Hey, guys." Kathrine greeted Danny and me. We said our 'hellos' and everyone took a seat. Hudson and Kathrine were on the other couch and Ava sat down right next to me.

"How was work?" Ava asked me.

"It was okay." I replied.

"What's it like working in a bowling alley? I bet it's a lot of fun."

"It's fun sometimes, most of the time though we just clean shoes and fetch stuck balls." I told her.

"Gross, I can't even imagine touching shoes that hundreds of people put their feet in." Kathrine cringed.

"I just try not to think about that." I said.

"Danny, you better have food!" Anthony shouted as he entered the house with Brian.

"Pizza rolls are in the oven!" Danny yelled back.

"Perfect." Anthony said as they finally appeared in the doorway.

Brian sat down on the couch with Hudson and Kathrine, and Anthony squeezed in between Ava and Danny on our couch.

We talked about random things until the oven went off.

"Pizza rolls!" Anthony and Hudson screamed together. They both jumped off the couches and ran into the kitchen.

"They are actual children." Kathrine muttered.

"I'm younger than both of them, yet I'm more mature than both of them put together." Brain shook his head.

"I better go help them before they burn the whole house down." Danny chuckled and disappeared into the kitchen.

"So, Paxton, are you excited for homecoming in a few weeks?" Ava asked.

"Oh, um, I'm probably not going." I responded. I've never gone to homecoming before and I didn't think this year would be any different. Penny didn't even go last year, because she didn't have a dress and we couldn't afford to buy her one. This year though she has been saving up a little money from each of her paychecks to buy a cheap, but nice dress.

"What? Homecoming is one of the best things about high school!" Kathrine exclaimed.

"I'm just not a school dance kind of person, I guess." I shrugged.

"Well, you should think about it. It's a lot of fun." Ava said.

"Ouch! Hot! Hot! Hot!" Hudson frantically ran back into the living room. He had his mouth wide open and we could all see his chewed up pizza rolls inside.

"I told you to let them cool down first." Danny groaned.

"You can't put pizza rolls in front of me and expect me to not eat them." He said back.

"I'll get you some water." Danny sighed and turned to go back into the kitchen. He returned with waters for everyone a few minutes later and everyone sat down again.

"Danny, can we play MarioKart?" Brian asked.

"I second that. I love MarioKart." Kathrine agreed.

"Yeah, sure, you know how to set it up." Danny said as he dropped a pizza roll into his mouth.

"Who else is playing?"

"I want to." Hudson said.

"Me too." Ava added.

Brian set everything up and clicked the tv on before searching for the remotes, "Danny, did you guys move where you put the remotes?"

"Oh, yeah my mom put them in the cabinet over there. She got mad we kept leaving them out." He pointed to a cabinet under the tv.

Brian retrieved the remotes and passed them out.

"I call being Princess Peach!" Kathrine claimed her character.

"We know, Kathrine, you call her every time." Anthony said from his spot on the couch.

"She's the best character and the best character should go to the best person here, which oh would you look at that, is me." Kathrine gloated.

I watched as everyone just rolled their eyes at her. The rest of them picked their characters and vehicles before starting a race. I was interested to see how the game was played, because we don't own any video games at my house. I watched in amusement as a group of twelve characters lined up at a starting line and raced each other for three laps around all different kinds of tracks. There were also power ups that helped and hindered the racers.

"Come on give me a red shell!" Hudson screamed at the tv.

"Ava, stop swerving in front of me!" Kathrine yelled.

"Stop being right on my butt and we won't have a problem!" Ava shouted back.

I laughed at their interactions and looked over at Danny. He was already watching me and smiled when he saw me staring. I turned back to the tv just as Hudson hit Brian with a shell.

"You son of a bitch! I was in first!" Brian yelled.

Hudson then passed his character and finished in first, leaving Brian to take second place.

"I hate you!" Brian exclaimed and threw a pillow at Hudson. It hit him square in the face, so Hudson grabbed it and threw it back at Brian. He was ready for it though and dodged it. The pillow than flew past Brian and smacked Kathrine in the head.

"Hey, leave me out of this." She said.

"Want to play again?" Ava asked the group.

"Yeah, sur—."

Brain was cut off by Anthony, "Hey, I just got a text that Kira's parents went out of town for the weekend, so she's having a party. We should go."

"She's having one tonight?" Kathrine asked.

"Yeah, I guess it was a real last minute thing. Can we please go?" Anthony pleaded.

"You just want to go, because it's Kira's party." Brian said.

"That's not the only reason! Come on, we never miss the chance for a party." Anthony insisted.

"Anthony's had a crush on Kira since last year." Danny leaned over to fill me in. I nodded in understanding.

"How could I not have a crush on her? She's gorgeous." Anthony stated.

"Yeah, but you're too chicken to ask her out." Hudson said.

"She broke up with her boyfriend like two months ago, I can't be a dick and just ask her out right after." Anthony defended himself.

"Two months is plenty of time to get over someone." Hudson retaliated.

"Well, putting Anthony's tragic love life aside, I could use a party." Kathrine said.

"And by a party you mean a drink?" Ava asked.

"Well, duh."

"Okay, let's go." Anthony jumped up. Everyone followed after him and went to the front to put on their shoes.

"Time for your first high school house party." Danny nudged my shoulder lightly and followed the others.

I sat on the couch in a daze. Everything just happened way too fast and before I knew it I was in Danny's car on my way to the party.

# Chapter 14

"Damn, I knew Kira had a nice house, but this is crazy." Hudson said from the passenger seat of Danny's car. He decided to come with us, because he didn't want to be stuck in the car with Kathrine and Ava as they talked about boys that would be at the p a r - ty.

I was seated in the back, but I could still see the huge house in front of us. The yard was enormous, but the staple of the property was the big, brick house. Our city had people from all social classes and Kira's house proved she was one of highest rankings.

"Honestly, it looks like a house for a celebrity." Danny agreed. He parked a little away from the house due to the high number of cars already lining the driveway and street. It was getting dark, but based on the loud music coming from Kira's house, the party seemed to have been still in full motion.

I got out of the car and stood next to Danny. A high school party was not my scene at all, so I had no idea what to expect.

"Just relax." Danny whispered in my ear after he noticed my tenseness.

"You said tonight would be chill. This doesn't look chill." I whispered back.

"I'm sorry, I didn't know there was a party tonight, but I promise it'll be fun." He said.

I looked into his eyes for a moment and was satisfied when they looked sincere. We eventually made it up to the house and the door was already open. Music and loud voices flooded out along with body heat.

"Should we wait for the others?" Danny stopped us before we entered.

"Hell no, they can meet us inside. I need a drink." Hudson answered and pushed his way inside.

Danny turned to face me, "Just stay close to me, okay?"

I nodded and followed him in the house. The temperature changed instantly and the air got thick with humidity from all the sweaty bodies. I didn't really take in my surroundings, because I was too focused on staying with Danny. He led the way until we entered the kitchen. It was slightly less crowded in there, so the air became more breathable.

Hudson was at the counter pouring drinks, so we joined him.

"I poured three, here." Hudson motioned to the three red solo cups in front of him. Danny picked one up and looked at the contents before taking a sip.

"That one is for you." Hudson nodded at the untouched cup and then at me.

"Dude, did you learn nothing from last time? He doesn't drink." Danny said.

Hudson slapped his palm to his forehead, "Shit, man, sorry I forgot."

"It's okay, just save it for one of the others." I yelled over the noise.

"Speaking of the others, there they are." Hudson pointed behind Danny and me.

"Kira's house is incredible!" Kathrine yelled once she got over to us.

"Yeah, are you sure you don't like her just for her money, Anthony?" Brian joked with his brother.

"No, I honestly didn't even know she lived here until tonight." Anthony responded. He sounded just as surprised at the massive house as the rest of us.

"Here, take this drink and then grow the balls to go talk to her." Hudson handed Anthony my unwanted drink.

Anthony took it without hesitation and downed the whole thing at once.

"Brian, come be my wing-man." Anthony said and started pulling Brian back towards the crowded living room.

"I never agreed to this!" Brian cried out as he was dragged away by his brother.

"Oh, I have to see this." Hudson laughed and followed after them.

"Why do I see this ending badly for Anthony?" Danny asked.

"Oh, because it definitely will." Ava laughed and poured herself a drink.

"Strip pong taking place by the pool right now between Weston and Richard!" Some girl ran into the kitchen and screamed. Some girls quickly filed out of the kitchen to go see the action.

"Richard Joyce is one of the hottest football players in the school." Kathrine turned to Ava.

"And he's playing strip pong? This I got to see." Ava replied.

The girls squealed at each other before running out of the kitchen just like the others have done previously.

"Want to go hangout in the living room?" Danny asked me, "Unless, you want to go watch two football players strip down for a bunch of girls."

"Living room sounds good." I replied.

We made our way into the living room and I noticed it wasn't nearly as packed as before. It also seemed like it was mostly guys at this point, which meant every girl heard of the strip pong game outside. Danny got us a spot on one of the couches, so we just sat for a while. People would occasionally come up to Danny and have a conversation before leaving.

During those times I mostly just listened, because I didn't feel comfortable talking to people I wasn't familiar with.

About an hour later, I was sitting next to Danny as he talked to some girl. I glanced around the crowded room and noticed Hudson on the other side with a girl. She looked heavily intoxicated and so did he. They soon started making out, so I turned my head. A few minutes later, I looked at the spot they were before and noticed it was occupied by different people now.

"Paxton, can you come with me to get a drink?" Danny suddenly asked me. I looked over at him and noticed the girl he was talking to was still here.

"Uh, sure."

"Great, see you later, Lucy." Danny dismissed the girl and quickly shot up from the couch. I followed after him into the kitchen. Once we made it, he looked over his shoulder to make sure Lucy didn't come with us.

"I didn't know how else to get rid of her." Danny sighed, "Lucy is super nice, but she doesn't take hints."

"So you don't really need a drink?" I assumed.

"No, that's just an added bonus." Danny smirked and poured himself another drink.

"There you guys are. We've been looking for you." Kathrine came up to us with Ava and Brian.

"Where's Hudson?" Ava scanned her eyes around the kitchen.

"He was hitting it off pretty well with some girl a little while ago." Danny responded, "Where's Anthony?"

"Kira invited him to join her for a joint." Brian said. He seemed to be holding back a laugh.

"Does he even smoke?" Kathrine questioned.

"Nope, that's what makes it so good." Brian finally let out his laugh, "He's gonna choke like hell when he takes his first hit. It'll be so embarrassing to do in front of Kira."

"Hey, that's your brother, be nice." Ava nudged him on the shoulder.

"Oh, come on, he's the one who agreed to go smoke with her. Plus, the job description of being a younger brother is to be annoying." Brian defended himself.

"Hey, Kathrine. Hey, Ava." A girl greeted.

"Hey, Violet. What's up?" Kathrine greeted back.

"There's a game of spin the bottle starting in the living room and we need more girls. You two wanna join?" Violet asked.

Kathrine and Ava looked at each other before shrugging, "Sure."

"Great." Violet said. The three girls then disappeared into the living room.

"Spin the bottle? Are we back in middle school?" Brian scoffed.

"You're just mad they didn't ask you to join." Danny commented.

"Damn right." Brian agreed, "I'm gonna go crash it."

I laughed along with Danny as Brian left the kitchen through the same door the girls just went through.

"Hey, I have to use the bathroom real quick. Will you be okay for a minute?" Danny said in my ear, so he didn't have to scream over the music.

I nodded and watched him leave. I looked around the kitchen. There were a few people lingering around having their own conversations that paid me no mind. I took a deep breath, I could survive on my own for a few minutes. Danny didn't have to be my babysitter just because I was new to the party scene.

I grabbed myself a red solo cup and filled it up with water from the tap. I wasn't really paying attention when I turned back around and I ended up lightly bumping someone with my shoulder.

"Oh, sorry—." I started.

"What's your problem, man?" An angry guy slurred at me. He was with two of his friends and they stopped to see what was happening.

"I'm sorry, it was an accident." I mumbled.

"Speak up, man, I can't hear you." The guy bellowed.

His loud voice and slur switched something inside me and I went into defensive panic.

"I said it was an accident!" I screamed defensively over the loud background noise.

"Hey, you ran into me, so you better watch yourself." The guy threatened.

"You were the one who told me to speak up." I said before I could stop myself. The confidence I had felt was immediately diminished after his eyes grew dark. My body deflated just like it had the other night with my dad.

"Well, aren't you just a tough guy." He stepped uncomfortably close to me. I was trapped between his big body and the sink. He reached forward and slapped my cup out of my hand. All the water spilled out onto my clothes, but I didn't even register it.

"Hey, get away from him!" Danny's voice pierced through the music. Hands suddenly pulled the guy hovering over me away and he was soon being dragged off by his two friends.

Danny quickly rushed over to me, "Paxton, are you okay?"

I couldn't answer him as all the feeling came back to my body and instead of being frozen in fear, I was trembling with it.

"Let's get away from all the loud music." Danny suggested and started pulling me away from the counter. I wasn't paying attention to where we were going in the house. The only thing I could feel was Danny's hand clasped together with mine as he yanked me around. I eventually registered going outside onto the patio and seeing a group of people huddled around the pool. Danny saw the large group too and guided me back inside. He then started opening every door on the first floor until he found what he was looking for, the basement.

We walked down the stairs and Danny searched for the light switch. He finally found it and the dark room illuminated. I didn't take much of it in other than the fact it was quiet and there was a couch, because Danny sat me down on it. He released my hand once we were seated, so I curled in on myself.

"Hey, Paxton, it's okay. You're okay. He wasn't your dad and he didn't hurt you. Everything's okay." Danny consoled me in a soft voice.

"I just barely bumped him and he went off on me." I whispered.

"I know, it's okay. It was just an accident."

"I'm such a joke." I said, suddenly feeling angry.

"What do you mean, Paxton?"

"I deal with my dad everyday when he's drunk. I've had to deal with him since I was born, so I'm used to it. I know what to do when he's angry and drunk. I can handle my dad without breaking down, so why can't I do the same for everyone else? I couldn't with Hudson and I couldn't just now." I confessed my confusion.

"I think, maybe, your dad is a constant in your life. Like you said, he's been this way since you were a child. That means you don't have to fear what could come out of the situation, because you already know. With Hudson and that guy, it was a new variable and you weren't sure of the outcome." Danny explained.

"I was just suddenly overcome with fear and I couldn't think of what to do." I unwrapped myself and sat up.

"You have every right to fear others when they threaten you, Paxton. You should never become immune to that." Danny put his hand on my knee, comfortingly.

"I know." I muttered and looked down at Danny's hand on my leg. We stayed in that position for a few minutes as I calmed myself down. I stopped shaking and got my thoughts back in order.

I looked back up at Danny and locked eyes with him. Neither of us said anything as we slowly leaned into each other until our foreheads touched. It should've felt strange, but it was like we just had the same silent desire and we both understood. I flicked my eyes down to Danny's lips and noticed his briefly did the same. I thought about how neither of us had spoken about our past intimate encounters and now we were in another one. I then thought about how I felt with Danny during these moments and I felt content with them. These moments were ours and we didn't need to talk about them, because we had a mutual understanding.

"Paxton?" Danny whispered and I felt his breath collide with my face.

I hummed in response.

"Can I kiss you?"

I almost said 'yes' without hesitation, but I couldn't help the need to clarify.

"Are you drunk?" I asked, my voice just above a whisper.

Danny let out an airy chuckle and his forehead bobbed against my own, "No, I'm not. I wouldn't want to forget one second of my time with you."

My body shivered at his confession, "Then, yes."

Danny didn't waste any more time before capturing my lips. Everything went numb for a few seconds, except my lips. I could feel every movement Danny's lips made on my own and it felt like the rest of my body was paralyzed.

Danny then licked my bottom lip with his tongue before gently biting down. My mouth opened slightly on its own accord and Danny took the opportunity. He found my tongue with his own and they danced in perfect rhythm. It was then that feeling in my entire body switched back on and the sensations were indescribable.

I pulled away first to catch my breathe, so Danny continued to place light kisses on my cheeks and forehead. He eventually stopped to look at me and I was right there with him. I gave him a small smile in which he returned with a big one of his own. It was then that I changed my mind.

I wasn't just content with Danny, I was the happiest I've ever been with him.

# Chapter 15

"We should probably go back upstairs." I said.

Danny and I were still on Kira's couch in her basement. After we kissed, Danny pulled me against him and I didn't have the willpower to stop him. I had my head on his chest and he had his arms wrapped around me. I enjoyed just laying there with him, but I knew a lot of time had passed.

"I doubt anyone is missing us." Danny answered as he raked his hand through my hair.

"Won't your friends come looking for you?" I asked.

Danny let out an airy chuckle, "No, they probably think I'm off making out with some girl."

"Oh," I muttered, "Does that mean they don't know?"

"Know what?" He asked.

"About this? You were off making out with someone. That someone just isn't a girl." I pointed out.

I couldn't see Danny's face, but I knew realization of what I was talking about set in.

"Oh, well, they aren't wrong to think I like girls. They just don't know girls aren't the only people I like." He explained.

"So you're—." I drew it out, so he could tell me himself.

"Bisexual."

I nodded against Danny's chest and reached for one of his hands. He let me take it and our fingers twirled around each other.

"Are you going to tell them?" I eventually asked.

"About being bisexual or about us?"

"I think it kind of goes together, don't you think?"

"Yeah, I guess it does." Danny said.

He was silent for a moment, so I flipped over to see his face.

He glanced down at me before letting out a breath, "I just don't know if I'm ready for that, yet."

"Do you think they won't be supportive?" I questioned.

"No, I think it'll be alright with everyone. I just don't know if I'm ready to put that part of me out into the world, yet." Danny squeezed my hand.

"Okay, I get that. So, am I the first one to know?"

"You're the first person to know." Danny put an emphasize on 'person'.

"What do you mean by that?"

"You know my step-sisters dog, Coconut?" He asked.

I nodded as I recalled him telling me about their dog dying a few months ago.

"Well, when I first realized how I felt, I needed to say it out loud to something other than myself. I wasn't ready to tell anyone I knew, so I told Coconut."

I stifled back a laugh for Danny sake, "Did it help?"

"As stupid as it sounds, yeah it did. It was like lifting a weight off my chest. It also felt like it was finally legit, like it was officially out there."

"I bet Coconut was super proud and happy for you." I smiled.

"Oh, he definitely was. His tail started wagging and everything." Danny chuckled.

I watched Danny's cheeks stretch up as he smiled and I couldn't help but smile too. I leaned up to peck his lips and we exchanged a few kisses before settling back down into a comfortable position. I didn't ask him any more questions about us, because I understood he wouldn't be ready for his friends and family to know about our feelings for each other. I was also in no rush to announce to the world that I liked Danny, because this moment was all I needed. This moment could keep me happy for years.

-:-:-:-:-:-:-:-:-:-:-:-:-:-:-:-:-:-

"Can someone tell me the character dynamic we see in Lady Macbeth in this scene?" Mrs. Anderson was asking the class another question about the play.

A few hands shot up around the room and Mrs. Anderson picked a girl in the front row. She gave a long, well-structured answer and I could tell Mrs. Anderson was pleased.

I glanced over at Danny and he noticed. He pretended to be falling asleep and I smiled. He then looked up at Mrs. Anderson before grabbing his phone. Once he was confident that she wouldn't spot him, he typed a message out and hit send. A few seconds later my phone vibrated on my leg. I pulled it out and kept it hidden under my desk.

Do you work after school? He asked.

No. I have to work all weekend, so I have the week off. I replied.

Danny looked at my message before typing back, Want to work on English after school?

Sure, which house?

My mom is hosting a gymnastic mom gathering at our house, so can we do yours? Danny asked.

Yeah, sure.

"Daniel, no phones in my class." Mrs. Anderson scolded Danny.

"Sorry, Mrs. Anderson." Danny's face turned apologetic quickly and he put his phone away.

She went back to teaching, so Danny looked over at me and smirked. I mouthed the words 'kiss-ass' at him, but his smirk just grew.

We sat through the rest of class and I was relieved when the bell rang. Danny and I walked to the parking lot and got into his car. He then drove us to my house and parked in the street after I suggested it. If dad came home, I didn't want to take any chances if he happened to be in a bad mood.

We got settled in and were just starting when Sidney, Penny, and Sadie came home. Penny had to work about two hours after school let out, so she would only be home for a little while. Polly still had her after school art club, so she would be home later.

"Since when are you better than us that you don't have to ride the bus home everyday?" Sidney asked as he took off his shoes.

"Since I became friends with someone who owns a car." I said back, playfully.

"Well, I'm just going to remind you that your car has four seats and I go to the same school as you. Use that information how you would like." Sid told Danny before jogging up the stairs.

"I'm going to do some homework before work. I'll be in my room if you need me." Penny informed us before following Sidney up the stairs.

"How was school, Sadie?" I asked my little sister as she sat on the floor, tugging at her shoes.

"Good, we got ten extra minutes at recess, because it was warm." She finally got her shoe off with one final tug.

"That sounds fun."

"I miss elementary school." Danny chimed in.

"Me too." I agreed.

"Everything was so simple back then. We didn't have to worry about grades or college." He sighed at the memories.

"Yeah, and the highlight of our day would be getting ten extra minutes outside for recess." I said.

"Good times."

"So, Shakespeare?" I asked.

"Yeah," Danny groaned, "Shakespeare."

Sadie ran off upstairs also, leaving Danny and I in the living room. We worked on English for about fifteen minutes before Danny got bored. He quietly set his pencil down and turned to me. I tried to ignore him at first, but he didn't like that. He leaned in and kissed my face right below my ear.

"Danny, we have to actually do our homework." I said and kept my eyes on my paper.

"Shakespeare is boring and why do something boring when I have someone not boring right in front of me?" He got closer to me, but I refused to look at him.

He reached up with his hand and gently pushed my face over, so I had no choice but to stare at him. I knew the moment our eyes locked, I would give in and I was right. His round, brown eyes looked into my green ones and suddenly our assignment didn't exist.

"My siblings are upstairs." I tried to hold onto any voice of reason I had left.

"And we're down here, so it's perfect." He replied. He didn't even give me the chance to say anything else before he crossed the short distance between us to connect our lips. His lips felt just as soft as the first time and I experienced the same sudden numbness I did during our first kiss. The numbness was shorter this time and I was glad, because that meant my entire body tingled with feeling.

I put my one hand on the back of Danny's neck to pull him closer to me and the other one got tangled up in his hair. I felt his hands placed on my back and they would occasionally grip my shirt.

We continued kissing, but neither of us tried to advance any further. We both seemed to understand that we wanted to preserve this stage of our relationship for a little while longer.

"Sadie, go bother Sidney or Paxton. I have to get my homework finished before work." Penny's voice rang through the house.

Danny and I quickly pulled apart and listened. A door opened before closing and tiny feet could be heard pattering down the hall. They stopped and another door opened.

"I have homework too, Sadie. Go play downstairs." Sid's voice said.

A door was shut once again and now the footsteps could be heard getting closer to the steps. Danny and I waited until Sadie could be seen at the bottom of the stairs.

"Penny and Sidney kicked me out." She mumbled.

"Why don't you watch some tv in here and we'll move to the kitchen?" I suggested.

"Okay." She agreed.

Danny and I collected all of our worksheets and set up in the kitchen.

I heard Sadie's cartoon turn on and turned to Danny, "We can't do that anymore."

"Do what?" Danny played dumb.

"You know what. What if Penny had Sadie come down here without us hearing?"

"It's fine. Nothing happened and you can't tell me kissing secretly doesn't give you some kind of rush." Danny whispered.

He was right. I did feel a thrill in making out in secret with my siblings upstairs, but I would never admit that to him.

"We just have to be careful. I don't want them knowing yet." I said.

Danny's face fell a little, "Will they not like it?"

"No, I think everything would go smoothly. I'm just not ready to tell them anything yet." I said.

Danny didn't reply, but I knew he understood. After all, we both had people we weren't ready to tell yet and I figured we could do it together when we both thought the time was right.

We continued to work on Shakespeare and every now and then Danny would peck my cheek. Every time he did I gave him a sharp look, but I couldn't help blushing a little.

After Penny left for work and Polly came home, I decided to start on dinner. We had all the ingredients to make sloppy joe, so I decided to whip that up. Danny decided to stay for dinner after he got a text from Jade that said all the gymnastic moms were still at his house.

"Can you pull out enough buns for everyone? It's almost done." I asked Danny and pointed him in the direction of the bag of hamburger buns.

"Putting me to work, I see." Danny teased.

"If you're going to eat my food, the least you can do is take out some buns." I joked back.

Danny grabbed five buns and placed them on the five plates I had set out. I scooped a serving onto each bun and placed them on the table.

"Dinner!" I yelled to my siblings. Sadie was the first one in since she was in the living room, but Polly and Sidney were not far behind. We all sat down and dug in. Polly talked about her art club and told me there would be a family showing of all their art at the end of the month. Sadie told us what she did with her ten extra minutes at recess and Sid complained about his teachers.

As I listened to each of my siblings talk, I studied Danny's reactions. He seemed genuinely interested in what they all had to say and he kept up with their conversations. He caught me smiling at him at one point and gave me a questioning look. I just shrugged it off and turned back to my sloppy joe. A few seconds later, I felt his leg brush up against my own which cause me to look back up at him. He gave me a smile before returning to Polly's conversation.

His leg though, stayed connected to mine.

# Chapter 16

"I will be placing you on lane twelve. Someone will be there shortly to put up the bumpers." I said to the lady in front of me.

"Thank you so much." She said before grabbing the shoes off the counter and handing them to her young daughter. She then turned her stroller around and rolled it towards the lanes.

I looked around the bowling alley for Hannah, but she was no where to be found. I was hoping I could get her to put up the family's bumpers, but it looked like I had to do it myself. I sighed and went to grab the long pole with a hook on the end. I made my way over to lane twelve and hooked the pole under the bumpers. With one big push, the bumpers clunked up and snapped into place.

"Um, excuse me, mister?" The young girl at the lane tapped my arm.

I looked down at her and smiled a little, "Yes?"

The girl looked back at her mom before turning to me again. Her mom was dealing with the toddler in the stroller and most likely told the girl to ask me her question by herself.

"My shoes are too big." She held the shoes up to me.

I gently grabbed them from her and checked the size. They were a kids eleven.

"I'll go get a size smaller, okay? I'll be right back."

The little girl nodded at me and bounced off towards her mom. I dropped off the bumper pole to its respective place and found a pair of shoes in children's size ten. I returned to lane twelve and handed the shoes to the girl.

"What do you say, Lacy?" The mom asked.

"Thank you." Lacy said to me shyly.

"You're very welcome." I responded. I then returned to behind the counter and started checking in the next set of customers.

It was Saturday and I was stuck working the entire day. Linda was out of town to visit her parents and I stupidly volunteered to pick up the extra shifts.

"Please tell me that was our last birthday party for the day?" Hannah joined me behind the counter.

I watched the group of kids with their parents leaving the bowling alley. I could tell the two parents that belonged to the birthday kid, because they were struggling to carry all the presents.

"Sorry, we have one more at three." I apologized to Hannah.

She slumped her body against the counter and groaned, "What age group?"

I checked the registry book on the counter in front of me and found the three p.m. time slot, "Twelve year old boy."

"Oh no, they're sometimes worse than the little ones, because they purposely like to cause trouble."

"Yeah, well just be happy you get to leave at six. I'm stuck here until closing."

"I can't believe you willingly volunteered to work extra." Hannah finally lifted herself from the counter.

"Linda has done so much for me, the least I could do was help her out for a weekend. Plus, I could use the extra money." I explained.

"Well, I better go clean the party room, so it's ready by three." Hannah searched the desk for the storage closet key. Once she found it, she lazily walked off.

I was about to clean some shoes that were piling up on the counter when my phone buzzed. I pulled it out of my pocket and read the message.

I'm thinking of going bowling later tonight. Know any good places?

I smiled at Danny's text and answered, I heard this place, Linda's Lanes, was good. If not for the bowling at least for the good looking staff.

It only took a few seconds for another message to pop up, I think I'll check it out then.

Danny and I texted back and forth a little more until the alley started to get busy. A lot of families came in with their young kids, looking for a fun activity. At three, the party arrived and I directed them over to Hannah. Then at six, Hannah clocked out, leaving me alone. At around nine, Danny walked in with Ava and Hudson.

"Hey, Paxton." Ava greeted me from the other side of the counter.

"Hey." I greeted all of them.

"Two hours each." Danny said. I rang them up at the register and told them the price. They all paid separately and I gave them each a pair of shoes.

"You guys sure like coming here a lot." I commented as I handed Hudson his shoes.

"Well, it's kind of the only thing to do here except the movies." Ava responded.

"Yeah, and the movies they're playing right now are shit." Hudson chimed in.

"Plus, I'm good at bowling, so it's fun to beat their asses." Danny laughed.

"Oh, shut up. If we ever get a laser tag or something in this city, I'll show you who's boss." Hudson punched Danny's shoulder.

"Whatever, go get the lane set up." Danny said back and shooed the two off.

Once they were gone, Danny turned to me, "How's your day been?"

I shrugged, "Pretty boring. We've only been slightly busy throughout the day. How about you?"

"Better now that I'm here." He smirked.

I rolled my eyes, "Shut up."

"Anyway, you want a ride home? I can wait till closing at midnight."

"You really don't have to." I tried just like I always do.

"Okay, great, so I'm taking you." Danny slapped his hands down on the counter before pushing off, "Now, I have some asses to go kick."

I chuckled and watched him join Ava and Hudson at the lane. I spent the next hour cleaning shoes and setting up games. The alley was starting to get pretty quiet around ten. Only half the lanes were filled and not too many new people were coming in. I was spraying down some tables when the door chimes rung from someone entering. I looked up towards the door and felt my stomach drop. Standing in the doorway, taking in the bowling alley, was none other than my dad.

I quickly made my way behind the counter. I felt like I needed that extra protection between my dad and me. Almost like the wood was some kind of barrier that would keep me safe. Dad spotted me at the counter and made his way over. I noticed his walk wasn't too staggered, meaning he was most likely only buzzed. I couldn't tell yet if that was a good thing or a bad thing.

I glanced over at Danny's lane and saw that neither him or his friends noticed that anything was going on. Another quick glance around the entire bowling alley told me the other costumers didn't notice either.

"Paxton." Dad greeted, flatly. My name didn't come out of his mouth slurred, so my prediction of him only being slightly intoxicated was correct.

"You can't be here." I said forcefully, but made sure to keep my voice down.

"This is a public establishment, so I actually can be here." He retaliated.

"If you are going to cause a scene, you can't be here." I grabbed onto the counter for support.

"I'm just here to visit my son at his place of work."

"What do you want?" I asked. There was no way he would be here if he didn't want something from me.

"I just want to talk. I went to that restaurant your sister works at earlier, but her boss and I got into a bit of an argument."

I shook my head at him and quickly pulled out my phone. Sure enough there was a text on there from Penny.

Dad came to my work again. He started yelling, so my manager kicked him out. He kept insisting I had his money. Did you take some out of his wallet again?

I shoved my phone back in my pocket and turned to my dad, "I don't have any of your money."

"One of you little bastards must have it. I had it when I went to bed last night and it was gone this morning." He said.

"You probably spent it on alcohol or lost it betting." I said back in a sassy tone, which was a mistake.

"Someone in that house stole my money and I demand to have it back!" Dad screamed.

Everyone's heads turned in our direction and I suddenly felt very small. I made eye contact with Danny and I watched as his eyes glazed over once he realized what was going on.

"Keep your voice down and leave." I tried to compose myself, but my voice came out shaky.

"I'm not leaving until you give me my money." He leaned over the counter towards me in a threatening manner.

"Mr. Meyers, I don't think this is the time or the place to be doing this." Danny was at the counter with us now. Ava and Hudson were still at the lane, but their game was completely forgotten.

"This is a family matter and who do you think you are to waltz over here and butt into our conversation?" Dad turned his attention to Danny.

"Once you screamed loud enough for the whole place to hear, it stopped being a private conversation." Danny said without skipping a beat.

"I want my hundred bucks back." Dad decided to ignore Danny and turned his glare back to me.

I felt my eyes go wide. One hundred dollars was a lot of money. I have never and would never take that much from my dad at one time, because the chance of him noticing was extremely likely. Plus, it was rare that he even had that much money on him at a time. He usually only got money by getting lucky in a bet or something, but then he would quickly spend it on alcohol.

"I don't have your money and you need to leave." I finally got some of my voice back.

"Then you better find out which of the little shits you call your siblings does have it and get it back to me. Or all five of you will have hell to pay." Dad threatened and grumpily walked out of the bowling alley.

I stood there in shock. My dad was an all around terrible person, but at least he had enough sense to know causing this big of a scene in front of the public wouldn't be good for any of us.

"Hey, Paxton." Danny called out gently. He reached for my arm over the counter, but I stepped back.

"I—I need a minute." I said and hurried to the locker room. I slid down against the lockers and sat there for what felt like an eternity. The past couple of months have been getting progressively worse and worse with my dad. He was growing impatient and started to lash out more than normal. He was like a bomb and his fuse was burning shorter and shorter with every given day. Eventually he would blow and it terrified me, because there was a million different ways that explosion could happen. I couldn't plan for his break and there was no way I could prepare my siblings for it either. It would just happen one day and we will just have to survive the initial shock and repair the damage.

I eventually pushed myself up and walked back to the front counter. The clock told me there was still an hour until closing. Danny was stationed at the counter waiting for me. I looked around and noticed Ava and Hudson were gone.

"I sent them home, so we could talk." Danny told me after he noticed my wandering eyes.

"Can we talk after closing?" I asked.

Danny looked hesitant to agree, but he nodded anyway. He then took a seat at an empty table. I tried to go about the rest of my shift normally, but it was hard. I could tell Danny kept an eye on me the whole hour, but I ignored him. At about five till midnight, the last pair of shoes were brought up to the counter. I followed the costumers to the door and locked it once they were out. I then grabbed the cleaning supplies and got to scrubbing the tables and floors. I would talk to Danny, but I had to keep busy while doing it or I just knew I would break.

"My home life was the last thing I wanted your friends to know about me." I muttered.

"Stop saying my friends, they are your friends now too." Danny said.

"They won't want to be anymore." My scrubbing of the table got more aggressive.

"Paxton stop." Danny ordered and grabbed my arm. He yanked the rag out of my grasp and threw it into the soapy water bucket.

"I need to clean." I tried to reach past him to get the rag.

He stopped me, "No, you are not going to pull the strong, older brother act in front of me. I'm not one of your siblings and you don't have to pretend to be okay all the time around me."

Danny's brown eyes bore into my murky green ones and everything came bubbling up. I flung myself into his arms and held on as tight as I could.

And he did the same to me.

# Chapter 17

I pulled away from Danny with tears in my eyes, but I refused to let them fall.

"One year ago he would never even think about showing up in a public place like this to cause a scene." I told Danny.

"What changed?" Danny asked me. He then guided me to sit down at the table I was previously scrubbing and I complied.

"I'm not sure. There's loads of things that could be ticking him off."

"Why does he think you or your siblings have his money?" Danny then asked.

I looked down at the table. I felt slightly ashamed to admit to Danny that I have stolen from my dad in the past.

"Hey, it's okay. You can tell me." Danny reached out and took hold of my hand.

I played with his fingers for a few seconds before taking a deep breath, "I have taken money from him before, but only when I needed it for food or when he already had stolen my money."

"It's okay, you don't need to justify why you do it. This time it wasn't you though?"

"No!" I quickly said, "Taking a hundred dollars at one time is careless. I would never take that much at once."

"Do you think one of your siblings did it?" He asked.

I sighed, "I would like to think they're smarter than that, but I honestly don't know."

"Well, let's finish cleaning up and then you can go home and sort it all out tomorrow." Danny stood up and pulled me along with him.

I put all the balls back on their racks and took out the trash as Danny mopped the floor. I kept telling him he didn't have to help me since he didn't work at the alley, but he would just wave me off each time. We eventually got done and I followed Danny to his car after locking the doors. We drove to my house in silence and I was grateful for Danny not trying to make conversation. He knew I had to have a few minutes to just think everything through and I appreciated his awareness.

Danny put the car into park in the driveway and looked at me, "You going to be alright?"

I looked at dads truck next to us in the driveway and then up at the house. It was completely dark which told me everyone was most likely asleep.

"I'll be fine. I just hope he didn't do anything when he got home." I said.

"Penny would've texted you if anything bad happened." Danny reasoned.

I checked my phone lock screen and it was still blank, "You're probably right. I just hate that I have to go in there like nothing happened. I hate that I have to go to sleep in the same house as him just a few rooms apart."

"Hey," Danny put his hand on my leg, "in the morning you can figure everything out, but for now you have to try to get some sleep. The situation will just be worse if you deal with it while tired."

"I know." I mumbled.

Danny gave me a knowing look before crossing his upper body over the middle console and cupping my cheek. He pulled me in for a short, but meaningful kiss. The tension I was feeling since the scene at the bowling alley suddenly melted away and I felt lighter when he abandoned my lips. I kept my eyes closed for a few seconds after he pulled away, because I knew opening them meant I had to leave Danny and face reality.

When I eventually did open my eyes, Danny was giving me a small smile, but it didn't reach his eyes. I could tell he didn't want to leave me either, but he also knew he didn't have a choice.

"Text me the minute anything happens, okay?"

"I will." I promised. I then pushed open the car door and got out. I said 'goodbye' to Danny and walked up to the front door. Once I was inside, Danny reversed out of the driveway and disappeared down the street.

I was about to turn the living room light on when I heard a soft snoring coming from the couch. I made out the body lying on the furniture and realized it was dad. It wasn't the first time he was too drunk, too tired, or too lazy to climb the stairs to his room. I walked over to the couch and glared down at him. He was laying on his back and his one arm was dangling off the side of the couch. It was strange to me how such a horrible man could look almost peaceful when sleeping. My eyes then wondered to the coffee table and I noticed a six pack of beer sitting there. Two of the six were open, but the rest were still tightly sealed in the box. I scowled at the alcohol and snatched the carrier and two bottles off the table.

I went into the kitchen and dumped all of the contents down the drain. Alcohol was the root of our issues with our father. If beer didn't exist, maybe dad wouldn't be as bad as he was. I knew it wasn't just the alcohol that made him a terrible person, but it definitely didn't help either.

I collected the bottles and went out the back door to our outside trash can. I didn't want to risk dad waking up and finding them in the inside trash. As I threw them into the bin, one hit the rim and went crashing to the pavement. It hit the ground and shattered into a bunch of pieces.

"Fuck!" I screamed. Even without it intoxicating dad, alcohol still caused me problems. I carefully collected all of the broken pieces and threw them into the trash can. When I shut the lid, I suddenly felt exhausted.

I entered the house and made my way upstairs. Sidney was asleep in his bed which meant nothing too bad happened with dad or else he'd be with the girls in their room. I was too tired to change out of my clothes and just collapsed onto my bed. I dozed off quickly, but had a restless sleep.

-:-:-:-:-:-:-:-:-:-:-:-:-

I woke up to a loud crash coming from downstairs, followed by Sadie's scream. I jumped out of bed and ran down the stairs and into the kitchen. Sadie was standing on the counter with the cabinet door open and dishes all over the floor.

"What happened?" I asked.

"I'm sorry, Paxton." Sadie's eyes welled up with tears.

I quickly stepped over all the plates and reached Sadie at the counter, "Hey, it's okay, Sadie. Just tell me what happened."

"I needed a cup, but the only clean ones were all the way up here." She explained. I looked over at the kitchen sink and sighed at the sight of all the stacked up dirty dishes.

"You could've woken me up to help you. Why are you up so early anyway?" I questioned.

"I heard Daddy down here earlier. I thought he was making us breakfast. He was gone when I came down." Sadie pouted.

"I bet he had somewhere to be." I said for Sadie's sake. I was secretly glad dad wasn't down here with Sadie. I can't even imagine what crazy things he would accuse her of regarding his money, despite her only being seven.

"Sorry I made a loud noise." Sadie apologized again.

I looked up at her on the counter, "It's okay. Luckily we only have plastic dishes and not glass ones."

I then picked Sadie up from her waist and brought her back down to the floor. She immediately started collecting the dropped dishes without me even asking. I smiled as I watched her. She was a good kid and I knew she would turn out alright when she grew up. I helped Sadie with the rest of the dishes and put them back in the cabinet.

"Where's your cup?" I asked once we were all done.

"I didn't get one." Sadie said, shyly. I chuckled at her and grabbed two cups from the cabinet. She then insisted on pouring the orange juice for both of us, even though I offered to do it.

"Want some scrambled eggs?" I asked Sadie once she was contently sipping on her orange juice.

"Yeah."

I pulled out the carton of eggs from the refrigerator and set up a pan on the stove. I was halfway through cooking the eggs when Sidney walked in.

"Eggs?" I asked him after he plopped down at the table. He looked tired despite being asleep when I arrived home yesterday.

He just hummed in response, so I added more eggs to the pan. Polly and Penny joined us a little later. Penny was dressed in her work uniform, because she had to work the opening shift.

"Dad came to the bowling alley yesterday." I announced once we were all eating.

"I knew he would bother you after my manager kicked him out of the restaurant." Penny groaned.

"Why does he think one of us stole one hundred bucks from him?" I asked.

"Probably because he lost it betting or spent it on beer and wants us to give him sympathy cash." Sidney piped up.

"No if he wants our money, he just comes right out and says it." Penny argued.

"Then one of his drinking buddies probably stole it off him when he was drunk." Sidney offered another reason.

"Maybe, but it still doesn't get him off our backs. He thinks one of us stole it and he's not going to let that go until he finds it or someone confesses." I said.

"I'm not confessing to something I didn't do." Penny said.

"Me neither." Sid agreed.

"Okay then we just have to lay low until this all blows over and he has something else to be angry at. Don't do anything that might set him off." I explained.

Everyone agreed and we finished eating our breakfast. Penny then left for work and I made Sid clean the dishes with Polly. I then spent the rest of the day working on some homework and watching television with my siblings on and off.

At around eleven at night, headlights illuminated the living room where Penny, Sidney, and I were watching television. Polly and Sadie were sent to bed about an hour ago, so we had the volume lowered.

"Welcome to your late night entertainment starring the Meyer siblings with special guest star, father Meyers." Sidney joked with sarcasm dripping from his words.

"Oh, be quiet and ignore him when he comes in. Maybe he'll leave us alone." I kept my attention on the tv screen even when the front door slammed open.

"Just the three people I wanted to see." Dad faked joy when he spotted us on the couch. He sounded surprisingly composed and sober.

"Go to bed." Penny tried.

"No, we are going to stay here until one of you fess up about stealing my money." Dad crossed his arms.

"None of us took your money." I finally turned my gaze towards him.

"I don't believe that for a second, but let's say I do just for fun. If one of you didn't take it, then who did?"

"Someone probably stole off you when you were too drunk to notice." Sid's voice showed no fear.

"Okay let's say that happened this time. What about in the past? I know for certain you have all taken money from me that adds up way over one hundred. I think it's time for some return." Dad's strange calmness was starting to worry me.

"We aren't giving you anything." I spat. I spoke harsher than I needed to, because dad was starting to freak me out. He was never this calm and I didn't know how to handle it. Danny told me I could deal with my dad, because his drunk episodes were the same. He would get worked up over something, yell at us, and then stomp out of the house or go to bed. Speaking to us civilly was new territory. My harsh words were almost like my unconscious trying to get him to react negatively, so the situation would feel normal.

"You will." Dad responded before walking up the stairs and disappearing into his bedroom.

We all sat on the couch in silence for a few minutes trying to collect our thoughts.

"What just happened?" Sidney was the first to speak.

"Why was he so calm?" Penny added.

"Because he wasn't drunk." I said, slowly.

"Okay, so what? He just suddenly decides to turn a new leaf and stop drinking?" Sid said.

"That'll never happen." Penny scoffed.

"He's not drunk, because he doesn't have any money." I informed my siblings, "That one hundred dollars was probably all the cash he had at the moment and now it's gone. He couldn't afford to buy a drink today."

"Well, then that's good. If he's this calm when he's sober, our lives might actually get better." Sidney was optimistic.

"It's doesn't work like that, Sid." Penny sighed. I looked at her and realized she was thinking the same thing as me.

"What do you mean?" He questioned.

"He's an alcoholic." She explained, "If he doesn't get alcohol soon, he'll lose it."

"And we will be the ones sitting here helpless when he does." I gulped.

# Chapter 18

"Sid, hurry up or you're going to miss the bus!" I yelled up to my brother. I was waiting in the living room with all my school items as Sidney was still upstairs. Penny took Polly and Sadie to the bus stop a few minutes ago after I said I would wait for Sidney to finish getting ready.

It's been two days since the money incident with dad and he hasn't come home. After his strange calmness that night, he left the next morning and hasn't reappeared yet. I'd be lying if I said I wasn't slightly relieved, because as long as he's gone there's no chance of him losing it on us.

Sidney came running down the stairs a few seconds later with his book bag on. I was about to tell him to quickly get his shoes on, so we could go, but I noticed his feet were already covered.

"Where did you get those shoes?" I asked as I eyed the brand new expensive looking shoes on Sid's feet.

"Oh, um, they are my friends. He let me borrow them." He answered. His face was suddenly overcome with panic and I immediately could tell something was up.

"Why would you borrow shoes?" I understood borrowing headphones, a video game, or even clothes from a friend, but not shoes.

"I just asked to borrow them for the week and he said it was fine. Can we go now?" Sidney seemed anxious to leave.

"Who let you borrow them?" I questioned.

"Uh, Frankie."

"You don't sound too sure about that." I squinted my eyes at him, suspiciously.

"I am sure! Frankie let me borrow them for the week." Sidney said.

"Why are you lying to me?"

"What?" His eyes bugged out of his head, "I'm not lying!"

"Yes you are. Come on just tell me how you got them. Did you buy them?" I fought to keep my voice gentle, so there was a higher chance Sid would open up and tell me.

Sidney sighed in defeat before nodding his head, "Yeah, I bought them."

"Okay, why couldn't you just tell me that you bought them?" I asked.

"I thought you would be mad that I spent money on shoes instead of food or the bills." He confessed.

"Hey, it's your money. You can spend it however you want. I do wish you would put some money towards the family, but I know you have in the past. A little splurge doesn't hurt."

I'll admit I was kind of upset that Sidney was spending his money on new shoes instead of family needs, but he's only fourteen. Plus, I've spent my whole life providing for my siblings so they wouldn't have to worry about the money issues. I don't get the luxury of buying anything other than the essentials, but that doesn't mean my siblings can't every once in a while.

"Okay. Sorry I didn't just tell you right away."

"It's okay. Now hurry up before we miss the bus." I said. We then both collected the rest of our things and left the house. We got to the bus stop just as the bus was rolling up.

-:-:-:-:-:-:-:-:-:-:-:-:-:-

"Danny we need to actually work on Macbeth." I said between my labored breath.

Danny invited me over to his house after school to work on our English assignment. We only had a few more scenes left before we had to write the essay and take the test. Then we'd be done with the assignment completely. We only worked for a few minutes in his room before we got distracted. He rolled the desk chair I was sitting on to his bed and dumped me onto the soft sheets before attacking me with kisses.

"We have the house all to ourselves and you want to read Shakespeare?" Danny looked at me in awe.

"Well, no, but we need to finish it at some point." I argued.

"We have plenty of time to finish. Just be here with me...in this moment...right now." Danny kissed a different part of my face between each phrase. He then didn't give me a chance to answer once he finished and kissed me hard on the lips. I responded by putting my hands in his hair and readjusted myself on the bed. Danny placed his knees on either side of me and moved from my mouth to kissing my neck. My hands left his hair and found the bottom of his shirt. I lifted up the fabric slightly before stopping to check Danny's reaction. He sat up completely, so I was looking up at him. He gripped the neck of his shirt and pulled it off in one swift movement. My eyes immediately shifted down to his now bare chest and I examined it with admiration.

Danny leaned back down to give me a sloppy kiss before whispering, "May I?"

"Yes."

Danny didn't wait another second before grabbing the bottom of my shirt and lifting up. I sat up on my elbows to help him pull it off easier and he discarded it on the ground next to his own. Danny then ran his fingers lightly across my skin from my chest to my stomach.

"You're so beautiful." He whispered. I looked him straight in the eye despite my blushing cheeks from his comment. I reached up and grabbed his chin, tugging him towards me. He complied and we became a mess of kisses and touches.

"That was way better than Shakespeare could ever be." Danny whispered from behind me. We were curled up on his bed under the sheets. He had his arms around me and our bodies were pressed together. Despite only making out with our shirts off, my body felt ecstatic the whole time. The slower and gentler moments with Danny always made me the happiest.

"Oh, shut up." I chuckled and snuggled closer to Danny.

I knew Danny told me to be in the moment with him, but as we cuddled in silence I couldn't help, but think back on Sidney and mine's conversation that morning.

"What are you thinking about?" Danny asked. It scared me how easily he could pick up on my mood changes.

"It's nothing. I was just thinking about something that happened this morning with Sid." I tried to brush it off, but Danny wasn't one to let things go.

"Hey, if it's bothering you then tell me. Did you guys have a fight?"

"No," I shook my head, "it's nothing like that. He just bought these new shoes that aren't cheap and when I asked him about them he lied. I knew he was lying so I called him out on it and then he confessed to buying them."

"What did he say?"

"He said he was borrowing them from a friend, but then said he bought them after I knew he was lying." I explained.

"Is it bad for him to buy new shoes?"

"No, I don't care if he buys new shoes. It's just that we normally put our money together for food and bills. Plus, it's weird of him to lie like that."

"He was probably just afraid you would get mad that he bought shoes instead of giving the money for family." Danny said.

"That's exactly what he said too when I asked him."

"Well, then there. He was just worried about upsetting you. And isn't he only like fourteen? He probably just wanted to impress his friends or a girl or something."

"Yeah, you're probably right." I dropped the subject.

"How has it been with your dad? Is he still on about the money?" Danny asked after a few minutes of silence.

"Actually, he hasn't been home in two days and I don't know whether that's a—." I stopped talking mid sentence as realization dawned on me.

"Paxton?"

"Oh my god." I sat up in Danny's bed.

"Pax, what is going on?" Danny sat up also.

"How much are a new pair of shoes normally? Like really nice new shoes?" I asked.

"I don't know, like sixty to eighty dollars. Paxton, what is wrong?" He grabbed my arm.

I shrugged his arm off and got out of his bed, "I need to go."

"Paxton, just calm down and tell me what you're thinking." Danny commanded.

"I think Sidney took my dad's money." I searched for my discarded shirt on the floor.

"What?"

"Think about it. Someone takes a hundred dollars from my dad and then not even a day later Sidney has the money to buy brand new, expensive shoes." I laid my thoughts out for him as I found my shirt and pulled it on.

Danny's eyes got wide, "Do you really think he would do that?"

"It would explain why he got so nervous when I asked him this morning and proceeded to lie to me about how he got the shoes."

"Okay, so what are you going to do?"

"I'm going to go home and ask him about it." I threw on my book bag.

Danny stood up from his bed and put his shirt back on too, "I'll drive you."

We descended the stairs and quickly got into Danny's car. When we pulled into my driveway, I got out after saying a quick 'goodbye' to Danny. He told me to stay calm as I was shutting the door, but I didn't answer. I ran up to the door and slammed it open.

"Sidney!" I screamed.

Sidney emerged from the kitchen with a confused look on his face. He opened his mouth to speak, but I beat him to it.

"Did you take dad's money to buy those shoes you were wearing today?" My voice held authority.

I watched as Sidney's confused look melted into a guilty one.

"Did you?" I questioned. I wanted to hear him admit to taking the money.

"Yes." He mumbled.

"Are you stupid! Dad caused us so much grief over that money and it's only going to get worse if he doesn't get it back!" I yelled.

"Paxton, I'm sorry I—".

"I don't want your apologies. You stood there this morning and lied to my face about those shoes. And you even came up with possible ways dad could've lost the money on his own when you knew damn well that you had it." I cut him off.

"I know, but—." He started again.

"What's going on in here?" Penny asked as she walked into the living room.

"Sidney is the one who stole dad's money." I informed her.

Penny looked confused and turned to Sidney, "Tell me he's lying."

"No, I'm not. He's the one who has been lying to us saying he didn't take the cash." I answered for Sidney.

"Sid, is this true." Penny wanted the verbal confirmation from Sidney just like I did a few minutes ago.

"Yeah, it's true." Sidney looked ashamed.

"Why would you do that?" She asked. Her voice was calm and collected compared to my loud and angry one.

"Riley said she liked guys who wore expensive things. I figured my shoes were old anyway, so it wouldn't hurt to get a new pair. I just wanted her to keep liking me. Saying that now, I realize how dumb that was." Sidney explained.

"Wait, Riley? As in the girl I caught you making out with at the lake party?" I asked.

Sidney nodded his head.

"Why do you care what a girl thinks of you? If she doesn't like you for you then that's her problem." Penny told him.

"I realize that now, but it's too late."

"What do you mean it's too late?" I asked. I was slowly starting to calm down.

"I already wore the shoes. The store won't take them back now." He elaborated.

"How much were they?" I asked.

"Seventy-five dollars. Why?"

"Do you have the extra money leftover?"

Sidney looked down at the ground, "Uh, I spent the rest to buy a necklace for Riley."

"Fuck, Sidney, what is wrong with you?" I groaned.

"Look I realize how stupid I was. I really am sorry."

"What are we going to do when dad finally comes home, wanting his money?" Penny chimed in.

I ran a hand down my face, "Okay, no one utters a word about Sid taking the money. We just continue to pretend none of us took it and that dad just lost it on his own."

Penny nodded while Sidney's face went pale. His eyes were focused over my shoulder, so I turned around. My whole body immediately froze and I heard Penny gasp from behind me.

"Too late." Dad growled.

# Chapter 19

"Wait, let's just talk about this like adul—." I tried to keep everyone calm, but dad was fuming.

"If that little piece of shit thinks he can steal one hundred dollars from me and not face consequences, he's got another thing coming." Dad cut me off. I could tell by the way he talked that he was still on his forced sobriety and was starting to lose it. The way his whole body shook was another sign. He was itching for a drink and I almost wished I didn't pour out all of the last of his beer the other night, because then maybe this conversation would happen differently.

"Look, he realizes how stupid it was to take your money, but he regrets it. Can't we all just move on now?" I knew it was a long shot of a request, but I had to try.

"This isn't the first time one of you have stolen from me! If you ask me, you've all had this coming." Dad pointed out.

I felt a little deflated, because he was right. I've been taking cash from my dad for as long as I can remember. I've just done it in tiny little increments, so there's no real harm. Sidney was reckless, took way more than he should've, and now we'll have to face dads wrath.

"Okay, what do you want?" I asked.

"I want my money back, dipshit." My dad said.

"I don't just have one hundred dollars laying around to give you. With bills and groceries, money is tight." I explained.

"I don't fucking care! Either he gives me my money or I'll teach him a lesson until he does." Dad threateningly stepped closer with his eyes locked on Sidney. I immediately blocked Penny and Sidney from dad's view by stepping in between them.

"Give me my money or move." Dad growled at me. I shifted a little in my spot, but held my ground. There was no way I was going to let the man in front of me hurt my siblings.

"No. He made a mistake and he feels bad about it. Just leave it alone." I said.

"I'm down one hundred bucks! How else am I supposed to get that money back?"

"Maybe you should get off your lazy ass and get a job." Sidney remarked from behind me.

"Sidney!" Penny gasped in shock.

Dad's eyes grew dark and I knew he officially lost the small amount of sanity I had been previously talking too. He tried to lunge past me towards Sid, but I held him back. I wasn't strong enough to hold him off forever, but it didn't matter. It turned out he only cared about letting his anger out on someone and I was someone. He stepped away from me and before I could register what was happening, he drew his fist back and connected with my cheek. I stumbled back a little and didn't really feel the pain until a few seconds after the punch was delivered. He didn't give me time to retaliate before punching me again. This time his fist connected to my left temple and my eyes unfocused for a second. I could then barely make out Penny screaming my name over the high pitched ringing in my ears. Another blow to my stomach caused me to crumble to the floor. I wanted to get up and fight back, but the ringing in my ears and my pounding head made it impossible.

Upon seeing that I wasn't going to get back up, my dad gave me one final kick to the stomach with his foot and moved over to Penny and Sidney.

"No." I groaned out from the floor. He ignored me completely and I watched in horror as he got closer to Sidney with his fist raised.

"Wait!" Penny yelled, "Here, I have thirty dollars on me. Take it for now and we'll get you the rest soon. Just please leave."

Dad eyed the money in Penny's outstretched hands. His whole body was still twitching from lack of alcohol. He glared at Sidney before swiping the money from Penny's hands.

"I want the rest back by tomorrow, got it?" He growled and swiftly turned around to leave the house. Once the door slammed shut Penny came running over to me.

"Oh my god, Paxton! Are you okay?" She kneeled beside me. I noticed her eyes were brimmed with tears. It hurt me to see her upset like this, so I forced myself up into a sitting position, despite the enormous amount of pain I felt.

"I'm fine." I groaned. I wasn't very convincing though, because the slightest movement of my body caused me to wince.

"I'm going to get some stuff to clean up the blood." She said and ran towards the bathroom. I squinted in confusion and brought my hand up to my face. I touched my temple and sure enough I felt a wet, sticky substance beneath my fingertips.

"Paxton," Sidney whispered from his spot in the living room, "I'm so sorry." He seemed to be frozen in place with shock.

"Hey, Sidney. It's okay and I'm okay. You made a mistake and now you can try and fix it." I forgave him. Part of me wanted to be mad at Sidney for causing all of this to happen, but the other part of me knew he regretted it and that he would never do something like it again. I figured there was no point adding to his guilt.

"But...he hit you." He whispered.

"Yeah, he did. He finally snapped, but I would rather take the punches instead of you."

"But it was my fault! I deserved to be punched, not you." Sid was starting to lose his composure as the shock melted away.

"Hey, Sid, it's okay. You didn't deserve this either, none of us did. Come here." I motioned him over with my head despite the pain. The ringing in my ears had gone down, but it was still buzzing quietly in the background.

Sidney slowly made his way over to me and sat on the floor, but he wouldn't meet my eyes.

"Hey, look at me." I demanded. Sid reluctantly made eye contact with me, "This is not your fault. It was just a matter of time until Dad would lose it. You can't blame yourself, okay?"

Sidney nodded his head just as Penny returned with wet wash clothes and bandages. She cleaned up all the blood trickling down my face and placed a bandaid on my temple.

"What are we going to do about the rest of the money?" She asked once she was all done.

"I'll get it." Sidney spoke up.

I looked at him in confusion, "How? You don't have a job."

"Just trust me, okay? It's my responsibility to make this right. I'll have the rest by tomorrow."

"Don't do anything illegal." I warned him.

"I won't." He rolled his eyes at me. I smiled a little at the playful interaction, but stopped when my cheek hurt.

I then spent the rest of the night cuddled on the couch with Sadie. We found her and Polly cowering under the bed in their room. Penny explained what happened to Polly, but I chose to save Sadie from all the grief and just told her I got a 'booboo'. I could tell she didn't fully believe me, but she didn't push it.

"Oh my god what happened to you?" Kathrine gasped when Ava and I arrived at the lunch table.

"Shit, dude, you look rough." Hudson chimed in once he looked up.

"Don't bother asking, he'll just tell you lies." Ava said as she sat down. She asked me during computer class what happened to my face and I told her I tripped over the sidewalk. She didn't believe me, but I refused to give her any other story.

"I fell over a raised part on the sidewalk. I'm fine." I told Kathrine and Hudson.

"Liar." Ava said, but I didn't respond.

"Who's a liar?" Brian asked as he arrived at the table with Danny and Anthony.

"Paxton. He says he fell on the sidewalk, but you don't get those kind of bruises from a face plant." Ava filled the boys in.

She was right. I had a huge bruise spread across my cheek that would only appear from a punch. It was also especially hard to convince Ava of the origins of my bruises, because she was at the bowling alley that night my dad caused a scene about his money. Her and Hudson didn't say anything about the incident at school after it happened which I can only assume was from Danny telling them not too, but I could tell Ava had her suspicions.

"Fuck man, who did you piss off?" Anthony whistled at the sight of my face.

"The pavement like I said." I muttered.

"Can we talk?" Danny asked me. He had yet to sit down at the table and one look at his face told me he was beyond angry. I knew he wouldn't take no for an answer, so I stood up and followed him out of the cafeteria. He led me to one of the less used bathrooms in the school. Once we were both inside, he checked for other boys. Once he was satisfied that we were alone he locked the main door from the inside and turned to face me.

"Your dad did that didn't he?" He asked. His tone was full of hate, but it wasn't directed at me.

"No."

"Don't you dare lie to me, Paxton." He walked closer to me and I instinctively stepped back.

Danny's face immediately softened after he noticed that he was scaring me.

"Pax, please just tell me the truth." He begged.

"Of course he did this Danny!" I said exasperated, "He's an alcoholic who went too long without alcohol and he snapped."

Danny closed the distance between us and gently ran his finger over my bruise, "I hate him."

"Join the club." I sighed.

"We should tell someone."

I pulled away from Danny, "No, we can't."

"He can't get away with hitting you like this."

"It was a one time thing, I swear. Plus, I'm not eighteen, yet. If anyone gets involved, I can't try to get guardianship over my siblings. We will all be separated." I explained. I didn't often talk about what could happen if anyone had their suspicions about my family. Luckily our city was big enough that most people didn't care about your own personal business, but it was a constant worry at the back of my mind that someone would figure it out. I hated to think what could happen if my siblings got taken away from me. They were my whole world and I couldn't lose them. Especially not before I was old enough to fight for guardianship if I needed too.

Danny looked at me with sad eyes, but I knew he understood. I spent my whole life protecting my siblings and there was no way I would let anyone take them from me without a fight. He gently cupped my cheeks while being mindful of my bruise and brought our lips together. The kiss was slow and gentle. He was silently telling me that he was here now to protect me the same way I protect my siblings. After the kiss he wrapped his arms around me tightly and I held on just as tight despite the discomfort the bruises on the stomach were creating. I nuzzled my face into his neck and breathed in his comforting scent. I smiled a little knowing he would be there to hold me in his arms and keep me safe.

# Chapter 20

I walked into the house after school with Penny, Polly, and Sadie. Sidney missed the bus which worried me slightly, but I had faith that he would turn up.

"Girls, go work on your homework." I told my sisters. I didn't want them downstairs when dad turned up for his money.

"I don't have homework." Sadie said as she took off her shoes.

"Then go play in your room for a little bit and then tonight I'll make meatloaf for dinner." I said.

"I love meatloaf." She exclaimed.

"I know." I chuckled and watched her go upstairs with Polly. Penny watched them go as well, so I turned to her, "I meant you too."

"The 'go do homework or go play' might work for them, but not me. I'm going to be right here when dad walks through that door." Penny told me. She then plopped down on the couch and pulled out some schoolwork.

"I just hope Sid gets here before dad does." I nervously looked through the window. Dad's truck and Sidney were both absent.

"Did he tell you where he was going after school?" Penny asked.

"No, I didn't even know he wasn't coming straight home." I joined her on the couch.

"He'll show up." She reassured me. I sighed and pulled out my own homework.

About a half an hour later the front door opened. Sidney came walking in with a bundle of cash in his hands.

"Where were you?" I asked.

"Getting this." He answered and lifted up the cash.

"How did you get that?" I asked next. Sidney was about to answer when the front door slammed open from behind him. Dad walked in looking calmer and less shaky than yesterday, meaning he used Penny's thirty dollars right away for booze.

"Where's my money." He asked.

Sidney turned around and held out the cash for him, "Here."

Dad grabbed it quickly and counted all the bills. Once he saw it was all there, he folded it and shoved it in his pocket.

"Next time just paying me back won't be enough." He threatened and left the house. Once he was gone all three of us slumped our bodies in relief.

"I'm surprised he actually left just like that." Penny said.

"Yeah, well, he likes booze more than he likes hitting us." Sidney joked.

"Not funny." Penny slumped back on the couch, but I could see a small smile on her face. I could tell she was relieved it was over for now just like I was.

"Okay, spill. Where did you get the money?" I asked Sidney again.

"I sold the shoes I bought." He admitted. I looked at his feet and it was then that I noticed his old, worn out shoes were back on.

"What about Riley?" I asked.

"I'm done trying to impress Riley. She either likes me or she doesn't." Sid shrugged.

"Well, I'm proud of you. You made a mistake and then you took it upon yourself to fix it." I praised my younger brother.

"Yeah, well I still feel like it wasn't enough to make it up to you. You still took all those hits for me." He pointed at my bruised face.

I thought for a second, "There is one thing you can do for me."

"What?"

"Make meatloaf tonight for dinner. I promised Sadie I would make it and now I really don't want to."

"Seriously." He groaned.

I laughed at his expense, "Do this and you will have made it up to me."

He groaned again, "Fine."

I then chuckled as he trudged into the kitchen to start on dinner. Dad would be back sooner or later most likely drunk, but I could handle him. The worst was over and I made it out with only a few bruises that would soon heal. Then, life could get back to as normal as my life could get.

-:-:-:-:-:-:-:-:-:-:-:-:-:-

"This movie sucks." Danny said as he pushed the pause button. We were on his bed watching a movie on his laptop.

"Yeah, there's like ten different plots at once and I can't keep up." I agreed.

Danny slowly closed his laptop and leaned over me to place it on his side table. On his way back over my body, he stopped. He grabbed the back of my neck and pulled me in for a kiss. Before long he adjusted himself so he was straddling me. We continued to kiss and he moved from my lips to my neck. At first he just placed small kisses all over my neck, but it soon turned into deeper kisses with occasional tugging at the skin.

"You're lucky your step-sisters always have some gymnastics meet your parents go to." I said as Danny continued to attack my neck with his lips.

He removed himself from my neck and put his forehead against my own, "I'm the luckiest guy in the world just because you're here with me."

I felt my cheeks turn hot from my blush, "Danny—."

I was cut off when he bit the skin right under my ear. My whole body shivered from bliss and my mouth fell open.

"Guess I found a sweet spot." Danny chuckled and sweetly sucked the same spot. Light moans escaped from my lips and I suddenly felt too hot for a shirt. I tugged on the hem of Danny's shirt and he took it off without complaint. He then did the same with my shirt. As he dropped my shirt over the side of the bed, his eyes widened at my stomach. I looked down and mentally smacked myself. I never told Danny about the bruises that littered my stomach from my dad. It's been almost a week since the whole incident happened, but the bruises were still faintly lingering on my skin.

"It's not as bad as it looks." I tried to play it off.

"Not that bad? Pax, it's been a week. If that's what the bruises look like now, I can't imagine how bad they were last week." Danny removed himself from on top of me and sat beside me on the bed.

"Okay, yes, it wasn't the best a week ago, but they barely hurt anymore. I'm getting better, so there's no use fussing over it now."

Danny reached out and lightly traced his finger over the bruise lines, "Why didn't you tell me it wasn't just your face?"

"I didn't want you to worry about me." I admitted.

"Of course I'm going to worry about you. What if he caused internal bleeding or something?" Danny kept staring at my stomach.

"He didn't." I put my finger under Danny's chin, so he would look at me, "I'm okay and it's in the past. Let's live in this moment right now, okay?"

"That's my line." Danny chuckled, softly.

"I'm borrowing it." I responded. I then brought Danny's lips back to mine and we shared a deep, passionate kiss. It only took a few minutes for things to get heated again and soon enough I was sprawled out underneath Danny as he didn't leave once inch of my stomach, chest, or neck not kissed.

I eventually mustered up the courage and strength to flip us around, so Danny was lying down beneath me. I started at his neck and worked my way down. I was peppering his collarbone with kisses when a loud moan emitted from his mouth and his body shivered.

"Looks like we're even on sweet spots." I airily chuckled. He responded with a breathy exhale and I kissed the spot again. Another moan erupted from his mouth and it was the best sound I've ever heard. I crawled back up to be face to face with Danny. He reached up and flipped a loose strand of my hair back to its place. We kissed again and Danny grabbed my hips. He turned us back over and placed his hands on my jean button.

"Can I?" He asked just like he always does. I smiled down at him and thought it over for a second. Danny made me the happiest I've ever been and he always focused on my needs and wants for our relationship instead of his own. It was time I did something for both me and Danny.

"Yes."

Danny grinned at me and moved to unbutton my jeans.

"You guys should really stop leaving your back door unlocked, someone might rob y—." Hudson said as he walked through Danny's bedroom door.

"Holy shit." Brian's voice was heard next.

Danny pulled away from me and I quickly sat up. I looked at Hudson and Brian standing in the doorway with confused and horrified expressions on their faces.

"Sorry...uh...we just—." Brian spluttered.

"We'll be downstairs." Hudson said and hurriedly rushed out of the room after yanking Brian with him.

After they were out of sight, I turned to Danny. His breathing was heavy and his face was frozen at the door.

"Danny?" I touched his arm and he whipped his head at me.

"I can't...this wasn't...this wasn't how this was supposed to go." He struggled to get the words out.

"What do you mean?" I asked.

"We were supposed to tell them together when we were both ready." He responded. It was the first time I've seen him really shaken.

"I guess now is a good time to be ready."

"But, I'm not ready." Danny whispered.

I looked at Danny with understanding and sympathy. He was fine with coming out to his friends as long as it happened on his own terms. Coming out was supposed to be something he could have control over and he felt like it was just taken from him.

"Hey, they didn't freak out too bad. They went downstairs instead of leaving which is a good sign." I consoled him. Danny didn't answer, so I found both of our shirts on the floor and gave him one. I pulled mine over my head and watched as he slowly did the same.

"Want to go talk to them?" I asked, gently.

Danny nodded, so I stood up and held my hand out for him. He took it and let me pull him through the house. We found Hudson and Brian at the kitchen table. They looked up at us when we walked in and then looked at our interlocked hands. Their stares caused Danny to squeeze my hand tighter and I led him to the table. We sat down with our hands still connected.

"So, you two are a thing?" Hudson was the first to speak.

I looked over at Danny. I knew he needed to be the one to give answers.

"Yeah." Danny's voice came out scratchy.

"Are you gay?" Brian asked.

"No, I'm bisexual." Danny answered. His voice was starting to sound stronger.

"And you?" Brian asked me.

"I'm not really sure, yet. I know I like Danny, but I haven't really thought past that." I answered truthfully. Danny is the first person I've really been attracted to, so I wasn't sure how I felt about others yet.

"How long have you been together?" Hudson asked.

"Since Kira's party." Danny responded.

"Cool." Hudson replied. His relaxed demeanor showed me that he wasn't really bothered by Danny and I. Brian seemed slightly more confused, but he didn't look disgusted or unaccepting.

"Cool?" Danny questioned.

"Yeah, cool. I mean I'm happy for you two." Hudson said.

"Uh, thanks." Danny said more like a question. He seemed taken aback by how unbothered his two friends were about what they just walked in on.

"Well, we came to see if you wanted to play video games, but if you're busy with other things." Hudson wiggled his eyebrows at us.

"No, that moment is kind of gone." I joked.

"Video games sound good." Danny said.

"I want the good controller!" Brian yelled and ran into the living room.

"Only if I get to pick the game!" Hudson followed after him.

"How do you feel?" I asked once they were both out of the kitchen.

"I don't know. Relieved, I guess. I still have to tell Anthony, Kathrine, and Ava." Danny sighed.

"Hey, they are happy for you, so you should be happy too. Plus, I also have to tell my siblings at some point."

Danny groaned, "Oh my god, I completely forgot I still have to tell my family."

I chuckled at Danny and cupped his chin. I pecked his lips before pulling him into the living room. We spent the rest of the night playing video games with Hudson and Brian. My favorite part was getting to watch Danny slowly relax again around his friends and really get into playing the game. A small chunk of the weight on his shoulders finally fell off and I was so proud of him.

# Chapter 21

"Then this is what we made the third week." Polly pointed to her clay figure on the table.

"It's really good, Polly." I said. We were at her middle school art club show and Polly was showing us all of her work.

"It's amazing. I think art is your calling." Penny commented. Polly smiled up at her and moved on to show us a little paper machete piece.

I looked around the crowded gymnasium. Kids were running around with their families showing their art work, but I was looking for one person in particular. I eventually spotted him at the door and waved him over.

"Hey." I greeted when he reached us.

"Hi, Danny!" Sadie said with excitement.

"Hi." He greeted back with an easy smile.

"What are you doing here?" Sidney asked.

"Polly invited me, remember?" Danny said.

Polly announced the art show at the dinner Danny was at earlier this month and she invited him to be polite. To our surprise, Danny accepted the invite and said he would come. I wasn't too convinced he would actually show up, but after he texted me this morning that he would be here, I knew he was serious.

"You're a little late, so you missed some of my pieces, but it's okay, we can just start over." Polly said and redirected us back to the beginning of the table. Sidney groaned, but I nudged him on the shoulder to shut him up. This art club meant a lot to Polly, so I was going to let her have her time to show us everything.

We walked with Polly through all of her art. She took the time to explain the week they worked on it, the inspiration for the piece, how she went about making it, and why it means something to her personally. I'll admit that about halfway through even I got a little bored, but I watched as Danny gave Polly his undivided attention. He seemed just as immersed in the backstory of each piece as she was.

"Students and families if I could just have your attention for a few minutes." A lady yelled over the buzzing of the crowd. Everyone quieted down and listened.

"I just want to thank you all for coming out and showing your support for not only your wonderful students, but also the art program in general. As another thank you, we have set up refreshments and small snacks in the cafeteria, so help yourself. Again, thank you and enjoy the art show."

"Can we go get some food?" Sidney asked. He was just about bouncing of the walls from boredom.

"We can once Polly is done showing us her art work." I said.

"I only have one more to show you. I saved the best for last." Polly told us and walked over to the end of the table.

"We had to paint an interpretation of the best and worst part of our lives. The point of the piece was to draw the bad part as the majority and the good part sprinkled in. That way, we could remember that even though we have terrible aspects of our lives, we also have good parts that overshadow the bad." Polly explained the painting.

I marveled at the canvas. The whole canvas was a gray room that was all torn up and destroyed. Tables and chairs were flipped upside down. Books and papers were littered through-out the room. The television had a cracked screen and there was shattered glass all around the floor. Everything was painted in black, white, and gray. The part that stood out was the five cocoons hanging from the ceiling. They were dark and murky in color just like everything else. Four of them were already hatched and one was in the process of hatching. Hatching from the one cocoon was a gorgeous brightly colored butterfly. Scattered throughout the rest of the trashed room was four more beautiful and vibrant butterflies. The butterflies were the only colored part of the canvas and they added a touch of magic to the painting.

"At first glance, you wouldn't think the cocoons would ever amount to anything good. But even in the worst conditions, beautiful butterflies will emerge from their temporary home and live their own free life." Polly explained.

I looked over at my younger sister in awe.

"It's beautiful, Polly!" Penny gasped and hugged Polly tightly. When she pulled away I noticed Penny had tears in her eyes.

"You are way too wise for your age." I settled for ruffling Polly's hair, because I was afraid I would lose it if I said anything else. Polly was the most down to earth person I knew and she was incredibly smart for her age, so I wasn't surprised she would think of a piece like this. It gave me a sense of comfort knowing my siblings thought of our home as an unfortunate setback in their life and not an already predestined doom.

"We can go get snacks now." She said lightly, despite the heavy feeling we all felt.

"Sounds good to me." Sidney said and booked it towards the cafeteria. We all chuckled and followed after him. I stayed back for a few minutes to look at the painting. Polly did an incredible job portraying our life and I definitely saw an art career in her future.

"What are you thinking about?" Danny asked from beside me. Once he noticed I wasn't following the others, he came back to join me.

"I think we should tell them." I said and finally tore my eyes from the painting to Danny.

"About us?" He asked to clarify.

I nodded my head.

"Okay." He searched my eyes for an ounce of uncertainty. When I didn't provide any he reached for my hand and gave it a light squeeze, "All of our friends took it well and I'm sure they will too."

"Anthony didn't." I reminded him.

Danny sighed, "Maybe not at first, but he came around."

I thought back on Danny telling the rest of our group about us. We decided that once Hudson and Brian found out, we needed to tell the other three before someone slipped up and said something on accident. So at lunch the next day we told Kathrine, Ava, and Anthony that we were together. They were all shocked at first, but Kathrine and Ava were happy for us. Anthony was another story. He stood up from the table and angrily walked out of the cafeteria. Brian wanted to follow him, but Danny insisted that he had to. Danny came back a little later and said that Anthony just needed some time to think about everything. I didn't push for a complete story, because I could tell whatever Anthony had said to him had hurt him. Two days later, Anthony rejoined the lunch table and said he was sorry for acting out and that he was happy for us.

"Do you think this is a good time to tell them? I don't want to ruin Polly's day."

"Hey, we can hold off if you want to." Danny told me.

I shook my head, "No, we need to tell them. Just not here. Can you come home with us after? I think it'll be better to tell them there."

"Of course." Danny gave my hand one last squeeze and let go. We then walked to the cafeteria and joined my siblings for drinks and snacks. We all joked around and laughed with each other. Polly told us a story about how this one kids ceramic project blew up in the kiln, because he left an air pocket, so everyone's project was ruined. I enjoyed the time with my siblings, because I couldn't help but feel like after I told them about me and Danny things would change.

-:-:-:-:-:-:-:-:-:-:-:-:-:-:-:-

"Who's turn is it to make dinner?" Penny asked as we all walked into the house.

"Sidney's, but I feel like cooking tonight." I said.

"I'm cool with that." Sidney said and ran upstairs before I could change my mind. I felt like I needed to be doing something until it was time for dinner, because I couldn't let myself have time to back out of telling my siblings. I made my way into the kitchen and knew Danny followed.

"What are you going to make?" He asked.

I looked in the pantry and refrigerator before answering, "We have enough frozen chicken tenders for everyone, so that wins."

"Can I help?" He then asked.

"Yeah, preheat the oven to 400 degrees Fahrenheit." I instructed. Danny went to deal with the oven and I poured out the chicken onto a baking sheet. We then sat in silence for the oven to heat up and once it did, I slid the platter in and closed the door.

"Now we wait." I sighed.

"It'll be fine, I promise." Danny said.

"You can't promise that, not really."

"Okay, you're right. I don't know how they are going to react, but I do know that they look up to you and love you so much. I really don't think this will ruin your relationship with them." He said.

"It's just so much scarier having to be the one to tell them. The way Hudson and Brian found out actually seems easier."

"Oh god, no. That was horrifying and Hudson teases me about it every chance he gets." Danny cringed at the thought.

"Yeah, you're right. I would be mortified if any of my siblings walked in on us."

"Plus, it's impossible to be upset when eating chicken tenders, so we'll be fine." Danny joked.

The oven beeped and I retrieved the tray of chicken. While we waited for them to cool, Danny helped me set up the table. I then dished out the chicken equally between all six plates and called my siblings down for dinner. We enjoyed the meal for the first few minutes before I looked over at Danny. He gave me a slight nod, which gave me the courage to speak up.

"I want to tell you all something."

Five pairs of eyes turned to me expectedly. My siblings eyes held curious looks and Danny's eyes were reassuring.

"Um...Danny and I...are, uh...together." It took me a while to get the words out, but once I did I felt relieved. I only felt relieved for a split second though, because I remembered telling them was only half of the equation. I was now at the mercy of their responses.

"Together?" Polly repeated.

"Yeah, like, you know, dating." I clarified.

"Since when?" Sidney asked.

"For about a month and a half."

"No." Sadie spoke up forcefully. We all turned to her and I noticed her face looked flustered.

"What?" I asked gently. Sadie was the last person I would guess would have a problem with me and Danny. I doubted she even really knew what relationships were.

"My teacher said boys get crushes on girls and Danny isn't a girl." She explained.

"Sadie, boys can get crushes on whoever they like. Same with girls." I said.

"Are you sure? My teacher knows like everything."

"Yes, I'm sure."

"Oh, okay." Sadie shrugged and bit into her chicken tender.

"Are you gay?" Penny asked.

"Maybe. I don't know. I've only ever been attracted to Danny." I explained.

"Doesn't that make you gay then?" Sid asked.

"Well, no. Sexuality is a spectrum and Pax just hasn't found where he lies on it yet." Danny answered for me.

"Where do you lie?"

"Bisexuality."

"What's that?" Polly asked.

"I like boys and girls." He replied.

"Well, you two dating finally explains it." Sidney said.

"Explains what?" I asked.

"Explains why he gives you rides everywhere and is always over here or you are always at his house."

"Friends hangout with each other too, you know."

"Not that much." Sidney remarked. Danny chuckled and I laughed with him. I felt good. My siblings took the news really well and even asked some questions to better understand the situation.

"Thank you all," I voiced, "for being supportive."

"Of course, Paxton. It doesn't matter who you like as long as they're good for you, which Danny seems to be." Penny smiled.

"Just who would've guessed it would be the pizza delivery guy." Sidney joked.

"I still can't believe the three of you like mushrooms." Danny cringed.

"I am going to force feed you a mushroom everyday until you stop hating on them." I threatened.

"I'll help, because mushrooms are amazing." Sidney offered.

"Hear that? You better watch your back." I said.

"No, you better watch out, because I have Polly and Sadie on my side, right girls?" Danny asked.

"Yeah!" Polly and Sadie both screamed. I laughed at the interaction and sat back. The hardest part for me was finally over and everything went smoothly. I wouldn't be completely relaxed though until Danny told his family. I knew his moms approval meant a lot to him and that's why they didn't know yet. I promised myself to be patient with Danny though, because he's been nothing but patient and incredible with me. We were taking this step by step together and all the possible hardships were worth it as long as I got to be with Danny.

# Chapter 22

"I heard this level is the hardest to complete." Brian said.

"Not with the two of us playing. I can't think of a better video game duo." Hudson replied.

We were all sitting around Anthony's and Brian's living room. Brian and Hudson were playing a video game and Anthony was giving them strategies. Ava and Kathrine were huddled close to each other on the couch looking at homecoming dresses. I was cuddled into Danny's side, playing with the tear in his jeans and Danny had his arm secured tightly around me.

"Paxton?" Kathrine asked as she looked up from her phone.

"Yeah?" I lifted my head from Danny's side.

"Have you decided on going to homecoming yet?" She asked.

"Oh, I don't know. It's really not my thing."

"So you're just going to make your lovely boyfriend attend homecoming all by himself?" Ava said.

I looked up at Danny, "Are you going?"

Danny nodded his head.

"Do you want me to come?"

"Only if you're comfortable coming." Danny squeezed my arm.

"Seriously? You finally have someone you can formally ask to homecoming and you aren't going to?" Kathrine questioned in disbelief.

"I don't think a big homecoming proposal is either of our styles, Kathrine." Danny said.

"Definitely not." I agreed.

"Ugh, fine, but you at least have to go, Paxton. I promise you it'll be fun." She said.

I thought it over for a second before nodding, "Okay, fine, I'll go."

"Yay! What colors are you two going to wear?"

"Colors?" I asked.

"Well, yeah. You have to match colors if you're going together." Kathrine explained.

"Well, I don't even have a suit to be honest. I've never needed one before." I confessed.

"That's perfect! You can come to the mall with Ava and me to get a suit when we go pick out dresses."

I looked back down at the tear in Danny's jeans, "Well, actually—."

"You can just wear one of my suits. I have a navy colored one that you'll look good in." Danny interrupted me.

I blushed a little and smiled gratefully at Danny. He knew I didn't have the money to go buy a brand new suit for homecoming and he saved me from having to tell everyone else that.

"What color are you going to wear then Danny?" Ava asked.

"I'm thinking my dark gray one." He answered.

Kathrine squealed, "Yes! Navy and gray are going to look so good together."

"I didn't know color coordination was such a big deal." I admitted.

"Only the girls think it's a big deal, but it's really not." Anthony said with his eyes still glued to the television.

"Color matching is everything if you're going to homecoming with someone. Otherwise it would look like you aren't there with anyone." Kathrine explained.

"It doesn't matter." Anthony said back simply.

"Whatever, you wouldn't get it anyway. Oh, maybe I should go bold this year. What do you think about bright red, Ava?" Everyone drifted off back into their own conversations and I once again snuggled up into Danny's side. He played with my hair and we spent the rest of the night just hanging with our friends.

-:-:-:-:-:-:-:-:-:-:-:-:-:-

"This is impossible!" I groaned. I stood in front of the body length mirror in Danny's room and tugged once again at the tie around my neck in frustration.

"Have you never tied a tie before?" Danny laughed from his bathroom.

"I don't even own a tie, so no I haven't." I responded and attempted to tie it again, but it just resulted in one big knot.

"Here let me help you." Danny said, walking out of the bathroom. I eyed him approaching through the mirror and marveled at the sight. I turned around completely, so I could see him with my own eyes.

"You clean up nice." I commented. Danny's dark gray suit fit his body perfectly and the color complemented his skin tone nicely. His black tie that was somehow already all done up mixed well with the gray.

"You don't look too bad yourself, except for your knotted tie." Danny chuckled. He stopped in front of me and undid the knot. He then quickly tied it all up and smoothed it down on my chest.

"See? It's not that hard." He smiled.

"Speak for yourself." I muttered.

"Navy really suits you." He placed his hands on my hips.

"Oh, does it?" I smirked.

Danny hummed in content, "You look hot."

I responded by pulling his face towards my own. Our lips crashed for a hard, hungry kiss. I moved my hands to Danny's hair as we kissed and ended up messing it all up.

"Boys are you almost ready for pictures?" Danny's mom yelled up to us from downstairs.

"We're coming!" Danny yelled back once he pulled away from me. He turned to look in his mirror and groaned, "Now I have to go style my hair again."

"Not sorry." I said, coyly.

Danny just gave me a fake frown before disappearing into his bathroom again. He returned a few minutes later with his hair all combed through and styled.

"Ready for awkward pictures?" Danny asked.

I nodded and followed Danny downstairs. His mom and step-dad were in the living room snapping pictures of Amber and Jade. They looked really pretty in their dresses. They had a completely different style of dress, but they somehow still complemented each other really well.

"Oh, you two look so handsome!" Danny's mom complimented once she looked at us.

"Thanks mom." Danny replied. I could tell he was embarrassed by his mom fawning over him.

"Danny go get in a picture with your sisters." Danny's step-dad told him.

Danny joined Amber and Jade in front of the fireplace and his mom snapped about a million pictures.

"Okay, Paxton go join them." She motioned for me to go over.

I awkwardly joined Danny and his step-sisters at the fireplace. We took a few pictures before Amber and Jade got out and Danny's mom wanted a few of just the two of us. Danny put his arm around my shoulders in a friendly way to take the pictures. Danny still hasn't told his family about us, so to them I was just Danny's friend who needed a suit and ride to homecoming.

"Okay, we need to go or we'll be late." Danny eventually said to his parents.

"Okay, are you picking anyone else up on the way?" His mom asked.

"No, just the two of us as long as the twins still don't need a ride." He answered.

"No, Liv just texted that the limousine will be here in a few minutes for us." Amber said.

"I still don't get why your friends wanted a limousine for homecoming." Danny remarked.

"It'll be fun! You're just pressed, because you're not going in a limousine." Jade said.

"My car works just fine and it's cheaper." Danny said lightly.

"Okay enough. Go before one of them throws their high heel at you." Danny's mom joked.

We said our 'goodbyes' and left in Danny's car.

The ride was silent for the first few minutes, but I eventually spoke up, "Do you think you'll want to tell them soon?"

"I really want to tell them, but I can't bring myself to actually do it." Danny admitted.

"I'll be there for you through it all." I promised.

"I know. Um, can I actually tell you something?"

"Yeah, of course."

"When I first realized I liked girls and boys I thought I was lucky."

"What do you mean?" I questioned, confused.

"Well if I still liked girls then maybe I would just end up with one and I would never have to tell anyone I liked boys too."

"That's not really how it works, Danny."

"I realize that, but I still had hope, you know?" He sighed.

"Yeah, I get it. It would probably just be easier to end up with a girl." My voice sounded deflated. Danny's confession made me feel slightly guilty. If we weren't together then he wouldn't have to worry so much about telling his family about us.

"Hey, don't think that." Danny put his hand on my leg as he drove, "I've never been happier than with you. I don't care how many people I have to tell as long as you're there with me."

I smiled at Danny and watched as we pulled into the schools parking lot. It took a few minutes to find an open spot, but once we did we got out and went inside. The air was already hot and sticky from everyone's body heat.

"Let's go find everyone." Danny said in my ear, so I could hear him over the loud music.

We weaved through people until we eventually spotted our friends. They were on the dance floor jumping around with their arms flailing more than actually dancing.

"Hey." Danny greeted.

"Hey! Wow, you guys look amazing." Kathrine complimented.

"Thanks you do too." Danny replied.

Kathrine was wearing a slim, bubblegum pink dress that showed all her curves. Ava's dress was also tight fitting, but didn't pop out as much with its dark maroon color. Anthony and Brian were dressed in simple black suits, but Hudson had a bright green suit on.

"What's with the green suit?" Danny asked Hudson.

"Girls get to wear all these bright colored dresses, so why can't guys wear colored suits? You know gender equality and all that shit." He responded.

"And by that he means his grandma got it for him and he couldn't say no." Brian laughed.

"Oh, shut up. Everyone knows it's impossible to say 'no' to your grandma." Hudson argued.

We all laughed and went back to dancing. I stood there stiffly for the most part, because I felt weird dancing. Danny noticed and came over to me.

"Want to go get some punch?" He asked.

I nodded and followed him out of the loud gymnasium. We found the drink table and poured ourselves some punch.

"I wish you would loosen up and enjoy yourself." Danny said.

"This just isn't really my scene." I said.

"I know, how about we stay for another hour or two and then we'll leave." He suggested.

"Okay."

"But the offer only stands if you have some fun the rest of the time we're here." He added.

"Screw you, but fine." I agreed.

Danny smiled and grabbed my hand. He pulled me back to the others on the dance floor and started dancing. I slowly loosened my body and joined him. We swayed back and forth to the music for a few more hours. The only time we were interrupted was for the committee to announce homecoming king and queen. I recognized the king as a football player and Danny said the queen was a popular volleyball player he knew.

"Do you want to get out of here?" Danny whispered in my ear around midnight.

"I don't know. It's not like I'm having the time of my life here, but I'm not really excited to go back home either." I replied. It was true that I didn't really like going home lately. It's been pretty normal since Sidney repaid dad, but I couldn't help and feel the tension that loomed over all of us. We were all constantly on edge, just waiting for dad to come home one day and lose it beyond repair. I just had this gut feeling it was bound to happen soon.

"Want to stay at my house tonight?" Danny asked.

I looked up at him to see if he was serious and he was, "Are you sure?" I've never stayed overnight at Danny's house before.

"Yeah, I wouldn't have asked if I wasn't."

I thought it over before nodding, "Okay."

We said our 'goodbyes' to all our friends before leaving. Hudson dog whistled at us as we left the gymnasium and called out something along the lines of 'don't stay up too late' which caused me to blush. When we got to the car Danny rolled all the windows down, so we could enjoy the silence of the night and the crisp, cool air of fall.

"In the morning." Danny suddenly said.

"What?" I looked over at him in confusion.

"I want to tell them in the morning." He clarified. I realized he was talking about telling his family about us.

"Okay, as long as you really want to." I said and watched his face for any signs of backing down.

"I do. It's time." He said.

"Okay, I'll be right here with you until then and after." I promised as we pulled into his driveway.

Danny took the key out of the ignition and turned his body to face me. I gave him a small, reassuring smile which he returned before taking a deep breath.

"I love you."

# Chapter 23

"I love you."

The three words rattled around inside my head as I tried to make sense of them. They were just three tiny words with no real power when said separately in different contexts, but strung together they were one of the most powerful phrases to exist.

I loved Danny. I loved Danny since he stood up for me against my dad at the bowling alley. I loved Danny, but I was afraid my idea of love was wrong. My whole life had been nothing, but experiences that had skewed my perception of love. I thought fathers were supposed to love their children, but my dad hadn't. I thought mother's were supposed to love their kids so much that they could never leave them, but my mom was gone. I thought you were supposed to love your siblings for the advice and guidance they give not because you depend on them for your survival. All the love I had and hadn't received in my life made me question if what I felt for Danny was the right kind of love or my minds own manifestation of my messed up idea of love.

I looked at Danny on the other side of the car. His eyes were big and round and despite the darkness around us it seemed like his entire body was glowing. The air around us was silent, but my head was screaming those three words at me over and over again.

After my few seconds of silence Danny gave me a tiny nod of understanding. My eyes were beaming with love for him, but my mouth refused to speak. We got out of the car and made our way up to the house. Every light was off which told us Danny's parents were already asleep.

"Amber and Jade are staying over a friends house tonight, but they will be home in the morning when we tell them about u—." Danny said as we were taking our shoes off, but I cut him off.

I tugged on Danny's shoulder to turn him around and then gave him a long, hard kiss. He quickly reciprocated with his own lips and grabbed my hips. I deepened the kiss and clung onto the back of his shirt like my life depended on it. He slowly started guiding us in the direction of the stairs all while continuing our kisses. We clumsily made it up the stairs and into his bedroom several kisses later. He pulled away from me completely to shut the door quietly.

"We have to be quiet, my parents bedroom is at the end of the hall." Danny said once he turned back towards me.

"Yeah, yeah, whatever." I said boldly and closed the distance between us once again. Our lips crashed together and we took turns taking off each others suit jackets and ties until we were both just in shirts and pants. My legs soon ran into the end of Danny's bed. I fell back onto it and Danny came with me. He hovered over me a loving hunger in his eyes and attacked my neck with kisses. I tugged on the top buttons of his shirt and watched as he sat back to take it off. He then helped me with my own and dropped it beside the bed. He started kissing up and down my torso before finally resting his lips on the skin right below my ear lobe. My body shivered in bliss at the contact and he continued sucking at the same spot until I was completely relaxed beneath him.

"Can I?" He whispered in my ear. His fingers were tracing the button on my suit bottoms.

"Yes." I breathily answered.

Danny unbuttoned my pants and slid them down my legs and then tugged them off completely. He then stood up off the bed and did the same with his own. We never broke eye contact the entire time and neither of us said a word. Once his suit pants were off he climbed back on the bed and hovered over me. He kissed me slowly and gently before finally touching me through my boxers. I let out low moans as Danny continued and he kept kissing me to muffle them. Danny eventually replaced his palm with himself after asking permission. His hips rolled against my lower half and I occasionally met him halfway by lifting my hips up. The feeling was pure bliss, but I could tell we both wanted more.

"Can I take these off?" Danny stopped for only a moment to ask me.

"Yes." My voice was weak, but I was sure.

He slowly took of my boxers and then did the same to his own. We stared in each others eyes for a few seconds, communicating silently. Danny then leaned in and connected our lips before reaching down and taking me in his hand. A loud moan erupted from my throat and he quickly kissed me to muffle it from his parents ears.

He continued for a little while before looking deep into my eyes, "Do you want to?"

I thought it over and smiled up at Danny, "Yes."

He kissed me once again and got us both ready.

"Wait." I whispered as he positioned himself.

He immediately stopped and gave me his full attention. I looked into his brown eyes and sighed contently. My love for Danny wasn't skewed. My feelings were the realest with Danny, so there was no way what I felt was anything, but right. I needed Danny, all of Danny, but I couldn't lay here and let myself have him until I told him how I truly felt.

"I love you, too."

Danny's eyes softened and he gave me the biggest, most genuine smile I've ever seen. He closed the distance between our lips and we shared our most passionate kiss yet.

We then spent the rest of the night together as one and proved our love to one another in ways stronger than words.

-:-:-:-:-:-:-:-:-:-:-:-:-

I woke up to light breathing on my neck. As my eyes blinked open, soft light from outside was filtering into the room. My senses came back to me slowly and I felt Danny's arms wrapped around my body and his chest pressed up against my back. Then the memories of last night came flooding back and I smiled to myself. I slowly turned myself around in Danny's arms so we were face to face. I admired his facial features for a few minutes until they slowly fluttered open.

"Good morning." I whispered.

Danny yawned, "Morning." His voice was still groggy from sleep.

We laid there just looking at each other for a few minutes as we both woke up fully. We were in a perfect little bubble of comfort and we didn't want to leave. Eventually the sound of voices from downstairs filtered up through the cracks in the door.

"Do you still want to tell them today?" I asked as I pushed a strand of Danny's hair out of his face.

"Yes. No. Yes, I have to." He replied.

"Okay, do you want to go now?" I asked.

Danny sighed and pulled me closer to him, "Let's just stay here for a few more minutes."

I nodded and kissed Danny's forehead before snuggling back into his arms. We laid there until we heard Amber and Jade's voices downstairs also with Danny's mom and step-dad. As we got out of bed, Danny gave me a pair of his sweatpants and a t-shirt to wear. He then slipped on shorts and a hoodie before turning to stare at the door. I stood slightly behind and waited for him to make the first move. After a few moments he walked to the door and twisted the handle. The door opened and I followed him downstairs to the kitchen.

"Good morning! How was homecoming? Oh, hello Paxton. I didn't know you were staying the night." Danny's mom greeted. She was at the table with Danny's step-dad. Amber and Jade were at the kitchen counter pouring cereal.

"It was good and Paxton staying the night was kind of a last minute thing. I figured it would be fine." Danny answered.

"Of course it's fine, honey. We have plenty of cereal or I think we have some bagels if you would rather have that, Paxton." She offered.

"Cereal is fine, thank you." I said, but I made no move towards the counter.

I watched as Danny took a deep breath before speaking, "I actually needed to talk to all of you about something."

All four of them turned to Danny, "Yes, honey?"

"Um...I've actually, uh, wanted to tell you this for quite some time now, but um I wasn't ready, but I am now, so uh...I'm bisexual." Danny's voice was shaky, but he maintained eye contact with his mom the whole time.

"Bisexual?" Danny's step-dad asked.

"Yeah, it means, um, I like girls and boys." Danny answered.

I looked at everyone's expressions and saw mixed feelings. Danny's mom looked slightly taken aback, his step-dad looked confused, and Amber and Jade to my surprise were just looking straight at me with realization already on their faces.

"I love you." Danny's mom suddenly blurted out.

Danny looked at her confused, "What?"

"I'm sorry, I'm just a bit disoriented, but you know that I love you no matter what, right?" She clarified.

"I know, mom." Danny smiled and went over to give her a hug.

"You're going to end up marrying a girl though, right?" Danny's step-dad said once they pulled away from each other.

"What?" Danny faced him with confusion on his face once again.

"Well you can experiment with your fantasies in your own time, but in the end you'll have to end up with a girl."

"Um, why?" Danny questioned.

"Well, because that's more natural. Plus, if you ever want to have kids you'd have to be with a girl." His step-dad said.

"Being with the person you love is what's natural. And liking boys isn't a fantasy, it's my reality." Danny was starting to get defensive.

"Have you ever been with a boy? How do you know you actually like them?" He asked in an accusatory tone.

Danny whipped his head around to look at me, "Actually, I have."

Danny took a few steps back to meet me and grabbed my hand. He then turned back around to see everyone's reactions.

"You two?" Danny's mom gasped.

"Yeah, Paxton and I are dating." Danny said.

"Well, that's—." Danny's step-dad started, but he was cut off by Amber.

"I had a feeling there was something going on between you two." She said with a knowing look.

"Yeah, me too. We're happy for both of you." Jade added.

Danny smiled at his step-sisters and I did the same. I knew their support for Danny over their own father meant a lot to him.

"Girls, you can't possibly think that's natural." Danny's step-dad spoke up.

"Dad, who cares about natural? Danny is happy and that's all that matters." Jade said.

"Plus, Danny just stood here and told us all the truth about who he really is. We should be so proud and happy for him." Amber added.

Danny's smile towards his step-sisters grew and their dad decided to be quiet. He knew he was outnumbered in this situation and plus his opinion of us didn't really matter to Danny as much as his mom's did.

"I love you, Danny, and I'm happy for you. Paxton, you seem like a great young man and I'm not surprised Danny has an interest in you. He always has a way of picking the best people to include in his life." Danny's mom told us.

"Thank you, ma'am." I said, kindly.

"Thanks, mom." Danny said again and smiled.

"Do you two have any plans for the day?" She asked.

"I actually have to get Paxton back home." Danny answered.

"Okay." She nodded. She got up and crossed the room to get to Danny and me. She hugged him once again and I heard her whisper in his ear that they would 'talk more later'.

When they pulled away, Danny led me out of the room and towards the front door. We completely forgot about breakfast, but neither of us were really hungry anyway.

"Are you okay?" I asked.

Danny nodded, "Yeah, I actually am. I got my mom's and the twins support and I'm sure my step-dad will come around. He's just a little reluctant to change at first."

"I'm proud of you." I smiled.

Danny leaned in to give me a chaste kiss. We then got our shoes on and left in his car. We arrived at my house and I found it strange dad's truck was in the driveway, but I was too happy that I brushed it off.

"See you tomorrow." I said as I opened the door.

"Yeah, see you. I love you." Danny said.

I stopped and turned to give him a kiss over the console, "I love you, too."

I then got out of the car and made my way up the driveway.

# Chapter 24

As I walked into the house I was greeted by the sound of shuffling and objects being moved around. I then took in the surroundings of our living room and felt my eyes widen. The entire room was trashed from floor to ceiling. Our coffee table was flipped upside down, the couch was tipped on its side, and the television was pulled from the wall. Books from our shelves were thrown all over the floor and every frame on the walls were crooked. I even spotted our mail scattered on the floor with every envelope ripped open. One object stood out though. Placed perfectly undisturbed on the flipped over coffee table was a six pack of bottled beer. I then immediately knew who was responsible for the destruction and my happy mood from the morning diminished.

"Hello?" I called out.

I heard a grunt come from the kitchen, so I made my way across the trashed living room and into the kitchen. I was surprised to see the kitchen was a mess just like the living room. Our table was turned over, every chair was on its side, and every single cabinet door was open. The oven, refrigerator, and microwave were also wide open.

"Dad?" I called out to the man who was anxiously and angrily looking through the cabinets. I watched as he ignored me completely and tossed every dish over his shoulder onto the floor.

"What the hell are you doing?" I tried again.

He finally turned to face me and his eyes looked panicked.

"Where did you hide the money?" He asked. He sounded anxious which worried me, but I was more concerned with how he sounded drunk this early in the morning.

"What money?" I decided to play dumb.

"Don't pull my leg right now, boy. I need all the money you got." He said.

"I can't do that. Just tell me what's going on." I stayed calm.

"I was down at Stevie's last night like normal and a few guys came in wanting to play pool. We made bets and I smoked them the first game, but they insisted on doing double or nothing. We played again and those sons of bitches hustled me. I told them I'd be back with the money by noon." He explained. As he explained himself his tone went from panicked to angry.

"How much do you owe?"

"Five hundred."

I gaped at him, "Why would you bet five hundred dollars?"

"Because I thought I could crush those poor bastards. Now tell me where your stash of money is. I only have an hour left." Dad told me.

I shook my head, "No way. I'm not giving you five hundred bucks. We have bills to pay for this month and it's mine and Penny's money." When I mentioned the money also being Penny's I briefly wondered where she and my other siblings were. I then remembered Penny had work early this morning, but the other three should have been home.

"I am your father and you live under my roof, so when I want money, you give me it." Dad's eyes turned cold.

"Might be your roof, but I still pay the bills. I can't afford to give you five hundred dollars right now and honestly, I don't want to." I said.

Dad took a threatening step towards me, but I didn't back down. He then growled and turned back to looking through cabinets.

"I'll deal with you later, but right now I need to find this money." He said.

"You aren't going to find anything." I said more confidently then I felt. Since I went to homecoming last night I couldn't bring my saved up money with me. I hid it underneath Sidney's mattress, because I figured dad would think to look under mine and not his if he ended up searching for it.

"I'm giving you ten minutes to tell me where it is or I will make you tell me." He threatened.

"I'm not telling you anything." I crossed my arms.

Dad walked towards me and got in my face, "Ten minutes and then this conversation won't be peaceful." He then shoved past me and made his way upstairs. I quickly followed him and watched as he slammed open the girls bedroom door. Sadie let out a scream and Polly gasped.

"Girls go downstairs now." I instructed. Polly and Sadie jumped out of their beds and rushed past me to run downstairs.

Once they were safely out of the room I whipped around to face dad, "The money isn't in here."

"Then where is it?" He spat and pulled all of Polly's sheets off her bed.

"I'm not telling you. Just stop destroying everything!" I picked up one of Sadie's stuffed animals from off the floor.

Dad went through everything in the room before deciding I was telling the truth that the cash wasn't in there. He then shoved past me once again and went across the hall into Sidney and mine's room. I followed him into the room and was shocked to see it empty. I wondered where Sidney could be, but I didn't have time to dwell on it, because dad was tearing up the room.

I watched nervously as he pulled out all of my clothes and threw them on the floor to look through the dresser drawers.

He got done with my side of the room and moved over to Sidney's side. I gulped as he neared his mattress.

"Wait! The money is in the downstairs bathroom." I lied.

Dad halted and faced me. He checked my face for a lie and I fought to stay neutral. I must have convinced him, because he sprinted past me to run down the stairs. I debated on grabbing the money and running out of the house, but I had no where to go and I would be on foot, so I refrained. Plus, I would be leaving Polly and Sadie with dad and I didn't want to do that.

I made it back downstairs right as dad was entering the bathroom.

"Polly and Sadie go in your room, lock the door, and start cleaning up. Don't come out until I call for you, okay?" I said.

"You piece of shit!" Dad screamed and I heard something shatter. I assumed it was the bathroom mirror as that was the only breakable thing in there.

"Now!" I demanded and pointed to the stairs. Polly and Sadie dashed up the stairs and I heard their door shut.

"I tried to be civil, but you gave me no choice." Dad said as he rounded the corner back into the living room.

I didn't even have time to register what he was doing until his fist had already connected with my nose. My head whipped back from the contact and pain shot through my entire face.

"Fuc—." I didn't even have time to finish the word before another fist slammed into my cheek.

"Where is the money?" Dad screamed.

I stayed silent and waited for the next blow. It came within seconds and the force knocked me off my feet. As I laid on the ground in pain, dad started kicking my stomach and sides. I yelled out in pain and just tried to shield my face with my hands and my stomach with my legs. After a few more seconds of kicking I mustered up enough strength to slide my right leg out and knock dad off balance. He fell onto one knee and grabbed onto the coffee table leg for support. I then watched as he eyed the six pack of beer bottles, neatly packaged and unopened on the upside down table. To my horror, he gripped the neck of one of the bottles and swung it around towards me. I moved to shield myself, but the bottle still connected with the side of my face and shattered into pieces against my temple. I cried out in pain as glass and beer went all over me. I then felt the blood starting to trickle down my face.

"Tell me where the money is, now!" Dad growled.

"No." I managed to groan out.

Dad responded by grabbing another bottle and smashing it on the top of my head. The smell of beer filled my nostrils and the sticky substance covered my entire body. The alcohol also burned as it seeped into my open cuts. He did the same with two more of the bottles before I finally called for mercy.

"It's...under Sid's...bed."

My head was pounding and blood was starting to drip into my already wet from tears eyes. My vision was also growing blurry around the edges and my whole body ached. I kept my body tense to maintain eye contact with dad. He seemed satisfied with my confession and stood up. He then stomped his way up the stairs. I laid on the floor in pain as I heard him shuffling around above me. His footsteps could eventually be heard descending back down the stairs and I could faintly make out the pile of money in his blood covered hands through my blurry vision. He took one look at me before scoffing and leaving the house.

Once the door shut behind him, I completely collapsed onto the ground. My breathes were hard and labored and I had just enough strength left to call Polly and Sadie down. They came down the stairs timidly.

"Paxton!" Polly yelled once she saw me and ran over to my side. She knelt down beside me with tears in her eyes. I could hear heavy crying coming from the other side of the room and I knew it was Sadie.

"Don't...cry, Sadie." I coughed out.

"He hurt you really bad, Pax." She sniffled.

"I know...it'll be...okay." I was starting to feel weak.

"What should I do?" Polly asked, frantically.

"Where's Sidney?" I asked. Penny was at work, so she couldn't help me right now and Polly and Sadie were too little to help me.

"He never came home last night. Penny thinks he stayed over a friends house." Polly told me.

My protective brother mode kicked in and I became worried about not knowing the exact whereabouts of Sidney, but my mind was too scattered to really focus on it.

"I need...Danny." My voice came out as a whisper.

"What?" Polly leaned in closer to me.

I felt my body shutting down and my eyes started to flutter. I took a deep breathe and mustered up as much strength as I could.

"Call Danny."

# Chapter 25

"Paxton, wake up. Come on, Paxton. Open your eyes for me." A voice slowly pulled me from my sleeping mind and back to r e a l i - ty.

My eyes slowly fluttered open, but they shut again quickly due to a bright light.

"Polly go close the blinds." The same voice as before instructed. It took me a few seconds, but I finally placed the voice as Danny's.

"Danny?" I croaked out with my eyes still closed.

"I'm right here, Paxton. Can you open your eyes for me?"

I slowly blinked open my eyes and I was happy there was no more bright light shining in them. My eyes adjusted to the dim room and I recognized it as my living room. It was still completely trashed and I was in the same spot dad beat me up in. The longer I was conscious, the more pain I could feel start to come back to my body.

"Everything...hurts." I groaned from the pain.

"I know it does, Pax. We're going to get you to a hospital." Danny said. It was then that I noticed he was kneeling on the ground behind my head, propping it up on his knees.

"No!" I immediately said, "No hospital. We can't afford it."

"Your head is seriously injured, Pax. You need a hospital." Danny said.

"I'm not going to a hospital. I just need a shower, some pain medicine, and sleep." My mind was starting to feel less fuzzy and I could form full sentences.

Danny looked into my eyes from above me and I struggled to do the same. My eyes didn't want to focus on him, but I wanted him to believe I was good enough to not need a hospital.

He eventually sighed, "Okay, I'll let you take a shower and then we'll see about whether you need a hospital or not."

With his consent I tried to push myself up into a sitting position with my hands. Pain shot through my entire body, but I managed to sit up by myself. I then analyzed the room more. It was completely trashed like before, but now there was shattered beer bottles everywhere. The broken glass covered all the floor space around me and mixed in was all the previous contents of those bottles.

"Polly and Sadie can you start cleaning everything up? Be careful of the glass and I'll be right back out to help after Paxton is in the shower." Danny said to my sisters.

I then scanned the room and found my two younger sisters in the corner. Polly was holding Sadie tight and both of them had old tears staining their face.

"Hey girls," I said from the floor, "I promise I'm okay. And I promise everything will be okay."

"I'm sorry we didn't help you." Polly sniffled.

"You helped by staying in your room like I asked, so thank you for that."

Polly and Sadie both gave me a tiny nod and left to get cleaning supplies. Once they were gone I slumped back down into Danny as my strength was starting to leave me.

"Let's get you up." Danny whispered. He hooked his arms around me and gently helped me to my feet. It was a slow process, but we eventually were both standing.

"Can you walk?" Danny asked.

"I think so." I replied.

"Okay, watch out for the broken glass."

I moved my one foot forward slowly and then the other, but stopped from the pain that shot up through my leg and into my stomach.

"It hurts."

"Okay, it's okay. I'll help you." Danny said. He then leaned down and put his arms under my legs and back. He hoisted me up and carried me bridal style through the living room. I linked my arms around his neck for support and shut my eyes.

As he carried me away I realized I was stuck helpless in a room full of broken bottles and Danny came to save me. He met me in the middle of all the mess and carried me away to safety. I realized Danny has done that for me multiple times since we met. My whole life was like being trapped in a room full of broken bottles with no way out. The room had one door that was locked and I didn't have the key. I believed all hope to escape was lost, but Danny was the missing piece. He was the key to getting out and every time I found myself stuck in that broken room again, Danny was right there to stand by me and help me find my way back out.

We made it to the bathroom and Danny gently placed me back on my feet. I stumbled a little from the pressure of supporting my own weight, but he held on to my shoulders.

"You don't seem to have any shards of glass in your skin which is a miracle, but you do have some pretty deep cuts that need cleaned." Danny said as he examined my face and neck.

"Can I see myself?" I asked. I wanted to see just how bad I looked.

"Um, Polly said your dad punched the mirror and it shattered." Danny said and motioned his head over to the mirror. It was in fact all broken from what looked like a fist and I vaguely remembered it happened.

"I still want to see." I said.

"Maybe after you shower." Danny suggested.

"No, now Danny." I became a little more forceful.

Danny sighed and led me over to the mirror. It was hard to see through the cracks, but I found a big enough one that would show my face.

I gasped. Staring back at me was a boy with big cuts all over his head and blood only now starting to stop oozing out from all of them. My hair was all bloody just like my face and I could see bruises starting to form all over. I had to grip onto the side of the sink for support, so Danny pulled me away.

"Do you want help with your clothes?" He asked.

I nodded. My arms were aching and I knew I wouldn't be able to move much from my stomach injuries. Danny gently grabbed the hem of my shirt and slowly pulled it over my head. Once my shirt was off, I looked down at my stomach. The bruises weren't formed yet, but I could feel them beginning to. Before helping me with my sweatpants, Danny turned the shower on to warm up the water. He then came back over to me and helped me slip out of my pants.

"I'll be right outside if you ne—." Danny began to say, but I cut him off.

"No, please stay." I begged.

Danny looked at me with sad eyes before nodding. He grabbed a towel as I removed my boxers and stepped into the shower. I left the curtain open slightly, so I could see Danny. I felt the need to keep him close to me. The warm water then hit my skin and I finally lost it. I backed up against the shower side and slid down it. I hugged my knees to my chest and my tears mixed with the shower water running down my face. Within seconds Danny was at the shower curtain in only his boxers. He climbed in with me and joined me on the floor. He hugged me tightly and whispered reassuring words in my ear. We sat like that for a while and Danny just held me as I cried.

"Can I wash your hair and face?" Danny asked after I calmed down a little.

I nodded and lifted up my head from my knees. He ran his fingers through my hair and I watched as all the bloody water swirled down the drain. We eventually got done cleaning up and Danny helped me out of the shower. I wrapped a towel around my waist as Danny went to get me some clean clothes.

"I brought a t-shirt, sweatpants, and a hoodie." He said as he reentered the bathroom. I glanced over at the pile of bloody clothes on the floor.

"I'm sorry about your clothes." I said to Danny. He lent me some this morning and they were all ruined.

"It's okay. Here put these on then I'll clean your cuts." Danny handed me the clothes. I slipped them on slowly and sat down on the toilet. Danny kneeled in front of me and put disinfectant on all of my cuts. I hissed at the pain, but didn't stop him. He finished up with the bandages and placed a gentle kiss on my forehead.

"How do you feel?" He asked.

"My stomach hurts, my arms ache, my face is cut open, and my head is pounding. I feel fantastic." I said, sarcastically.

"Do you think you need a hospital?"

"No, I just need some rest." I said and stood up. I wobbled slightly from the pain and Danny instinctively grabbed onto me. He led me through the house and up to my room. I laid down in the bed and Danny pulled the covers up over me. As I eyed Sidney's bed I remembered he never came home after homecoming and I got worried.

"Does anyone know where Sidney is?" I asked.

"Polly said he hasn't come home yet, but I'm sure he's fine. Just sleep and he'll probably be home when you wake up." Danny told me.

"What if he's hurt or something?" I sat up.

"You're the one that is hurt and you need to sleep." He lightly pushed me back down.

"Can you lay with me?" I asked.

"I need to go help Polly and Sadie clean everything up. If you're still asleep when we're done I'll come join you." He promised.

"Wait, I want to help clean up. It's not fair for you three to do all of it." I said.

"Paxton, for once just put yourself in front of everyone else. Now, go to sleep." Danny brushed my hair back with his fingers and kissed my head. He then left the room and I fell into a restless sleep.

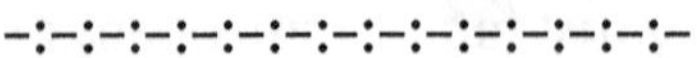

I woke up to hushed whispers coming from below me. I tried to listen, but my ears didn't want to focus on the words. I decided to get up, so I could find out who was talking. It took me quite some time to fully stand up and walk all the way downstairs from the enormous amount of pain my body was in, but I eventually made it. The voices quickly stopped as everyone noticed my arrival. Penny and Sidney were home and everyone was sitting in the living room.

"Paxton, you should still be resting." Danny said from the couch. I noticed the living room was back in order except for some beer stains in the carpet.

"I'm fine." I mumbled and joined him on the couch.

"I can't believe he did this to you." Penny said in a sad voice.

"It was bound to happen sooner or later." I shrugged it off. I could feel myself putting up a defense against everything that happened, because it would be easier to deal with in the long run.

"I should have been here to help." Sidney sounded guilty.

"Where were you?" I asked.

"I stayed the night at David's. I was going to call, but I forgot. I'm sorry." He explained.

"It's okay, I assumed you were just with a friend." I said.

"We can't just let him get away with this." Penny angrily said.

"We can and he will." I told her.

"What do you mean? He beat you up bad, Pax." She argued.

"Yeah and if we do anything we all get separated and I'm not letting that happen. Everything will get better in a few months when I'm eighteen and I can become a legal guardian if I need to."

"It's still not right." She huffed.

"It's in the past. Right now I'm just worried about this months bills. We are out five hundred dollars."

"I can help. I have some money saved up from working at the pizza shop." Danny offered.

"No way. I'm not taking your money." I immediately declined.

"I'm not saying I'll give you everything. Just a little to help."

"I said no. I'll manage on my own just like I always do. This is my responsibility." I said.

"It's all of our responsibilities. We're family, Paxton, and that means we will work this out together." Penny said.

"Yeah, you don't always have to be the only one looking out for us. We all look out for each other." Sid added.

"Okay." I agreed with my siblings, "we'll figure this out together."

"Together." They repeated with faint smiles.

# Chapter 26

"Four hundred eighty, four hundred ninety, five hundred." I counted.

"We did it!" Penny exclaimed.

"And with a few days to spare." Sid added.

"Yes, but I am paying them now, so there is no way dad can get his hands on it." I said and sealed the money in an envelope.

It was the end of the month and bills were due. Penny, Sidney, and I worked extra hard to earn back all the money dad took from us. Penny picked up extra shifts at the restaurant and I offered to take all of Hannah's remaining shifts for the month which she gladly accepted. Sidney ended up helping with the expense by mowing neighbors lawns and walking dogs.

"He never came home last night which isn't like him." Penny said.

"Good, maybe he's finally gone forever." Sid shared his optimism.

"I doubt it. He most likely just passed out somewhere. He'll be back." I dismissed it.

Ever since dad took our money he's avoided us. He comes in late at night after we are all in bed and leaves before any of us are up. And as much as I wanted to yell and scream at him for what he did to us and to me, him just ignoring us wasn't the worst thing.

A knock on the door pulled me from my thoughts.

"Hey." Danny greeted.

"Hey."

Danny walked into the house and took of his shoes, "How are you feeling?"

"Still a little sore in places, but I'm fine." I answered.

"Yeah, because instead of resting you went right back to work." Penny scolded.

"I rested for a few days, plus I needed to get back to work if we were ever going to make the five hundred back." I sat down on the couch with Danny.

"Did you?" Danny asked, putting his arm around me.

I leaned forward and grabbed the envelope off the coffee table, "All here."

"I'm proud of you. Even though your dad made your life hell this month, you still kept positive and got through it on top." Danny smiled at me.

"It wasn't easy, but we did it." I said, including Penny and Sidney on the achievement.

"Are you still up for hanging out with everyone tonight?" He asked.

I nodded, "Yeah as long as we aren't running any marathons or anything."

Danny chuckled, "Just a nice little party at Kathrine's house."

"Good. I'll be back sometime tonight and if there's any problems just call me." I told my siblings.

"There won't be any problems unless dad comes home." Sid said.

"Well, still, just call me if you need anything." I said as I got my shoes on.

"We will. Have fun!" Penny waved us off.

I pulled on a hoodie and left the house with Danny. As soon as we were out the door Danny attacked me with a kiss.

"What was that for?" I chuckled.

"No reason." He smiled.

I tilted my head at him, knowingly.

"I'm just happy you're alright." He sighed.

"I'm fine." I grabbed his arm, "it's going to take a lot more than a few punches and bottles smashed over the head to keep me down."

"Let's hope we don't have to find out just how much more." Danny said as he dragged me to his car.

We got in and he reversed out of the driveway. We made our way to the other side of the city and eventually pulled up to Kathrine's house. There were a few cars in the driveway already, but not too many. We parked and walked up to the door. It was unlocked, so we let ourselves in. Soft music and voices could be heard flowing throughout the house as we entered.

"Who's there?" Kathrine called out.

"Danny and Paxton!" Danny yelled back.

"We're in the back room!" Kathrine replied.

Danny led me through the house and into the big back room. We were greeted by Kathrine, Ava, Hudson, Brian, Anthony, and a few other people I barely recognized.

"How's the happy couple doing?" Ava asked, playfully.

"We are doing just fine." Danny said.

"Just fine?" Hudson repeated, "the way you two act around each other gives off more than 'just fine' vibes."

"Yeah you two act like you're already married." Anthony added.

"Give them time. They will be in the future." Ava said.

"They better be. If you two ever break up I won't believe in love anymore." Kathrine said, dramatically.

"I'm not too sure about marriage just yet," Danny hugged me from behind, "but I know I'm not letting this one go anytime soon."

Danny kissed the side of my face from behind and all our friends cooed. I shrugged him off from slight embarrassment and took a seat on the couch. Danny said his 'hellos' to a few of the people I didn't recognize before joining me on the couch.

"Do you want anything to drink?" He asked.

"Water, please."

Danny left me once again to get our drinks. He came back shortly with two bottles of water and some chips.

"Thanks." I said as I took the water.

"Of course." He replied.

"Paxton are you excited for next month?" Kathrine asked from her place on the armchair.

"What's next month?" I questioned.

"Danny told us your birthday was next month. You'll officially be an adult." She explained.

"Trust me it's nothing special." Anthony piped up.

"Oh shut up. I personally love being eighteen. I feel so much older and more responsible." Kathrine defended her age.

"Oh, yeah I haven't really thought about it." I said. That was a lie. I thought about turning eighteen a lot ever since I decided I would fight for guardianship over my siblings once I reached the allowed age. My siblings deserved someone who would put them first and look out for them without worrying about being taken away or harmed. I've been watching over them since we were little, so it only made sense to make it official.

"We should have a party." Brian suggested.

"That's a great idea!" Kathrine clapped her hands together in excitement.

"Oh no. I don't need a party." I said.

"Of course you do. You only turn eighteen once." She said.

"You only turn every age once, Kathrine." Hudson said as he took a sip of his drink.

"Okay, but eighteen is special. We're having a party." She decided.

"I would just accept it. She isn't going to back down." Ava warned me.

I nodded my head in defeat and laid my head on Danny's shoulder.

"I'll make sure they don't do anything too over the top." Danny whispered.

"Thank you." I whispered back, gratefully.

"Anyone up for a game of Twister?" Kathrine asked, shaking the box.

"I am! I'm like the human embodiment of a pretzel." Hudson jumped up.

A few others joined in, including Danny.

"Paxton, will you spin for us?"

"Sure." I grabbed the spinner and sat up on the couch. I flicked it and watched as it slowed to a stop.

"Left foot blue."

"Right hand red."

"Left hand yellow."

"Right hand blue."

I continued listing off the directions until everyone was one twisted mess on the mat.

"You are all going down." Hudson smack talked. Right as he finished talking, Brian's foot slipped and he came crashing down on top of everyone. The whole group fell into a pile.

"We all literally went down." Ava laughed and everyone laughed along.

"I won!" Hudson shouted.

"What? No you didn't. We all fell at the same time." Anthony argued.

"Yeah, but I was on the bottom on the pile which technically means I went down last, making me the winner."

"That's not how it works."

Anthony and Hudson continued to argue back and forth over who technically won as everyone else settled back into the furniture. Kathrine dimmed the lights and put on a movie. Danny grabbed a blanket and draped it over us. I snuggled in close to his side and sighed contently.

Just a few months ago at the beginning of the year I was wishing for this year to go by quickly and easily. I was living my life on autopilot and I didn't plan on taking control anytime soon. Then, I met Danny. We met for the first time due to pizza, but that English project, which we finished with an 'A', is what really allowed us to get to know each other. Danny gave me chance and became my friend then decided to continue being my friend even after finding out about my terrible home life. I managed life on my own before Danny, but he was the extra little piece I needed to actually start living.

It was then on that couch snuggled in Danny's arms, that I realized he was the only one I wanted to spend my life with. I wanted him to be there when I turned eighteen. I wanted him to be there for our graduation. I wanted him to be with me for everything. Danny was the one, my one.

And although life wasn't going to be easy for us, especially with my dad and us not having the same opportunities for our futures due to our different social classes, we would make it through together. In a few months I would be eighteen and would have to fight to be granted guardianship over my siblings. Danny might not understand all the hardships that process will take, but I was confident he would offer his support and wait patiently for me to get through it.

Our future together might be as scary and unpredictable as being in a room full of broken bottles, but we were in that room together and we would find a way out together.

So as I looked up at Danny and admired the way the soft television light illuminated his facial features perfectly, I came to a conclusion.

We could handle a few broken bottles.